PARANORMAL COZY MYSTERY

Lies & Pumpkin Pies

TRIXIE SILVERTALE

Sittin' On A Goldmine
Productions L.L.C.

Sittin' On A Goldmine Productions, L.L.C.

pr@sittinonagoldmine.co

www.sittinonagoldmine.co

ISBN: 978-1-7340221-4-8

Cover Design © Sittin' On A Goldmine Productions, L.L.C.

Trixie Silvertale
Lies and Pumpkin Pies: Paranormal Cozy Mystery : a novel / by Trixie Silvertale — 1st ed.

[1. Paranormal Cozy Mystery — Fiction. 2. Cozy Mystery — Fiction. 3. Amateur Sleuths — Fiction. 4. Female Sleuth — Fiction. 5. Wit and Humor — Fiction.] 1. Title.

CHAPTER 1

THERE'S NO REJECTION more poignant than that of a vending machine from the late 80s spitting out your money with brutality. If the temperature inside this fieldhouse ice rink wasn't subzero, I wouldn't be so desperate for hot chocolate. I catch my bill as it drops and carefully straighten each corner, taking special care to smooth out all the undesirable wrinkles and make my one-dollar bill as irresistible as possible.

Holding my breath, I gingerly feed it into the temperamental machine—for the third time.

Success!

The ancient contraption makes several questionable clicks and groans before expelling a paper cup which teeters on the metal grate landing pad.

I hastily steady it as molten cocoa sprays into the receptacle with surprising force.

Who knew getting a steamy beverage at the broomball arena could qualify as an extreme sport?

The dangerous transaction ends and I retrieve my drink. The rich chocolate aroma lifts my spirits and the heat against my mittens instantly warms me.

The rowdy pregame warm-up is well underway by the time I exit the extravagantly named "snack bar," which consists of three vending machines: sweets, savories, and hot chocolate.

Twiggy waves with uncharacteristic enthusiasm as I cautiously climb the wooden bleachers.

"Sit down. Sit down. You're gonna miss the face-off."

As a film-school dropout, I should warn you that no one will ever be able to utter the words *Face/Off* in my presence and not evoke an instant image of John Travolta and Nicolas Cage.

"So, what am I looking at here?" I gesture toward the aggressive display on the ice.

Twiggy was my grandmother's best friend in life, and is my sole employee at the Bell, Book & Candle Bookshop, which I inherited when Grams passed. I use the term employee loosely, since she technically works for free. She allows me to compensate her with entertainment, which usually features my natural clumsiness getting the best of me, or other forms of public humiliation. The fact that I successfully climbed the grandstand without slipping and spilling my hot chocolate seems to have displeased her.

She kicks one of her biker-boot-clad feet up onto the opposite knee and rubs her mittened hands on her dungarees as she exhales loudly. "Look, kid, it's a lot like hockey, but without skates."

Shrugging helplessly, I'm forced to remind her of a couple things. "Spoiler alert, I used to live in Arizona. Remember? Not a lot of hockey."

Twiggy shakes her head, and her severe grey pixie cut barely moves. "Yeah, I keep forgetting how much of life passed you by. Listen up, I'm only gonna explain this once. Ice rink. Two teams. Five guys and a goalie on each team. This is National League play, so, obviously, they're allowed to wear broomball shoes. The sticks are a modern version of the originals, which were actual brooms with the broomcorn bound tightly with cloth or, later, duct tape. The goal is to get that ball into the opposing team's net. Like hockey."

I scrunch up my face. "Doesn't hockey have a puck?"

"Geez, kid, the point was—object goes in net. Did that hot chocolate cook your brain, or are you always this dense?"

It's not clear how to answer that question without incriminating myself. So, ignoring her question, I return to my favorite pastime: watching Sheriff Too-Hot-To-Handle run around on the ice. If I'm lucky, maybe he'll take off his helmet and I can drool over his tousled blond hair as it falls into his eyes.

That's right, my sort-of-boyfriend is the team captain for the Pin Cherry Harbor Abominables.

A foghorn blasts, and the teams clear the ice.

The overly enthused voice of the announcer crackles from the speakers. "Ladies and gentlemen, and all you little Whisk Leaguers, welcome to the National Broomball Alliance National Championship!"

Something about that title feels as though it was approved by the Department of Redundancy Department. The sport doesn't strike me as one with a big PR team. I almost ask Twiggy about the Whisk League, but when an inordinate number of kids in numbered jerseys start banging on the plexiglass with wild abandon, I go with the obvious.

The announcer continues, "Tonight's match between the Pin Cherry Harbor Abominables and the Koochiching Arctic Arrows will decide the best team in the country!"

The crowd—and, surprisingly, there is an enormous one—roars and stomps their feet against the wooden planks.

"The winner of tonight's match will go on to represent the United States of America in an exhibition match against the Canadian champions!"

The crowd cheers, "USA! USA!"

"That's right, ladies and gentlemen, our boys are going to show those Canucks how it's done! The exhibition match will be played in Montréal in front of the Winter Olympics selection committee. Our fellas are going to take broomball to the Olympics!" The crowd is on their feet. The obsession with this strange sport has deep and thunderous roots.

The players on the visiting team are announced first, and then comes the home team. Apparently, there's a song and everything.

However, I have to admit, when they announce team captain Erick Harper, I stomp my feet right along with the rest of the broom bunnies. If I'd ever learned that cool trick of sticking your fingers in your mouth and whistling loud enough to deafen most humans, I'd certainly be doing it.

The players take their positions on the ice, and the referee holds the ball in the air between the two players who are facing off.

Despite Twiggy's insistence that she wouldn't

offer any additional explanation, she happens to mention that these two men are the centers.

The ball drops and the brooms fly!

The play is exceptionally invigorating. Our boys are running down the ice, passing the ball back and forth, when a moose-size man from the Arrows checks our forward into the boards so hard his helmet comes off.

Erick, number 10, races across the ice and checks the Moose, knocking him backward with a shocking crash.

The referee's whistle blows, but the crowd is screaming for blood and the adrenaline on the ice is ready to deliver.

The two assistant referees join the fray and pull the men apart. Whistles screech and penalties are awarded.

Erick and Moose are sent to their respective penalty boxes.

Play continues with each team down a man.

The first half ends without further incident, and with the Abominables in the lead. Play during the second half becomes desperate, and two more fights break out.

"Why is Erick getting involved in so many fights?"

Twiggy beams with pride. "He's the muscle."

I have no complaints about his muscles but

don't understand what they have to do with the fighting. I say none of this to Twiggy; however, the look on my face must show my confusion.

"He takes care of his team. If the other team pushes his guys around, he pushes back, harder." Her bloodthirsty grin is unnerving.

"Oh, he's like the mother hen."

She snickers and slaps her leg. "Yeah, you be sure to say that to him, kid."

The game ends, and the Abominables take the title. Fans storm the rink to congratulate the players. The smell of victory is in the air, and there's a huge celebration on the ice.

I scan the sea of puffy jackets and stocking caps, but when my eyes land on number 10, there's no rejoicing.

Erick and Moose, helmets off, are having angry words and Moose has a handful of Erick's jersey.

Just when I think things couldn't get worse, short and squat Deputy Paulsen toddles out onto the ice, in uniform, to break up the fight. With her tendency to draw her gun at a stiff breeze, I sincerely hope she doesn't shoot Erick.

"I gotta get down there, Twiggy. You don't need to wait. I'm sure Erick can drive me home. Thanks for introducing me to broomball." I raise my hands and make little explosion gestures next to my head. "Mind blown."

She shakes her head and clomps down the bleachers to join the festivities.

My foray into ice-based celebrations begins with a stream of polite "excuse mes," but quickly devolves into a snowplow and shove strategy. When I finally break through the crowd, the view is less than desirable.

Deputy Paulsen is threatening to arrest everyone, and Moose and Erick are in an intense shoving match. Moose temporarily gets the upper hand, and Erick goes down hard.

"And stay down, Harper." Moose spits on the ice. "Out here, you're nothing but a punk. Your badge is useless in the rink." A trickle of angry spittle clings to Moose's thick black beard.

Testosterone and adrenaline swirl together to create a dangerous concoction.

The sheriff fires up off the ice, and a left hook lands hard on Moose's face.

Moose teeters backward and crashes down with a thud of finality.

Erick leans over the mountain of a man and shouts, "I don't need a badge to take you out. Nobody takes cheap shots at my team. You better remember that on and off the ice—if you know what's good for ya."

My eyes widen. I've never seen Erick so angry,

but his instinct to protect his teammates is no surprise.

Paulsen grabs his arm and drags him toward an exit. "You're drawing quite a crowd, Sheriff. You better quit while you're ahead."

The heat of the moment fades and his shoulders sag. It's clear that he's not proud of what happened, but when his young teammate with a broken nose, courtesy of Moose, slides over and pats Erick appreciatively on the back, I can hardly blame him for taking care of his guys.

Outside the tight throng of spectators, the ice is far more slippery than it looks. Apparently, those broomball shoes have some serious mojo. Within seconds of my renewed attempts to reach Erick, my feet are circling like those of a cartoon character, and I land abruptly on my backside. Lucky for me, I've built up enough padding back there to avoid any serious injury.

The commotion catches Erick's attention, and he wrenches his arm free from Paulsen's grasp. "Moon, are you okay? What are you doing out on the ice? A fragile desert flower like you shouldn't be mixing it up with these broomball hooligans." The tenderness in his blue-grey eyes reminds me of the gentleman lurking inside the Abominables' enforcer.

He carefully scoops me from the ice, and I

reach up to push his blond hair back from his sweaty face. "Congratulations. Moose will think twice before he comes after any of your teammates again."

Erick scrunches up his face and shakes his head. "Moose?"

"Oh, that's the nickname I gave the big guy you were fighting with."

"We weren't fighting. It's part of the sport."

"Whatever you say, Sheriff." I bend to retrieve my dislodged stocking cap, eager to cover my haystack of snow-white hair, and the slipping starts anew.

Erick steadies me. "Let me get that for you." He grabs the hat and places it on my head like a caring parent.

"Can you also give me a ride home, kind sir?"

He chuckles and pulls me close. "It'll cost you." His words are accompanied by a mischievous wink.

My tummy tingles. "I can pay. I'm a rich heiress, remember?"

He leans down and whispers warmly next to my cheek, "Money can't save you, Moon."

I struggle to get air in my lungs as my face turns a dangerous shade of crimson.

He points toward the entrance. "You can hang out in the snack bar. I'll come find you as soon as I get changed."

"Copy that."

His broad shoulders shake with laughter as he heads into the locker room.

What can I say? The phrase is one of the few things that "stuck" from my months of on-set experience in the fast-paced world of filmmaking. As a production assistant it was my job to do whatever was needed as quickly as possible, and "copy that" was the way to let the powers that be, on the other end of the walkie talkie, know that I was on top of things. If it ain't broke, don't fix it.

Erick is unusually quiet on the drive from the fieldhouse to my bookstore, and my natural snoopiness fails to see the benefit of patience. "What's up? Aren't you happy your team won the championship?"

He nods and taps his thumb rhythmically on the steering wheel of his squad car. "Yeah. The guys worked really hard this season, and they deserved the title. But, now that the thrill of the win has faded, I'm feeling a little foolish for letting Klang get the best of me."

"Who's Klang?"

A soft grin spreads across Erick's face. "The guy you called Moose."

"Oh, that guy." I want to mention how shocking it was to see him in a fistfight, but clearly his own conscience is already berating him enough. "Is he gonna be all right? I mean, he'll definitely have a black eye. But other than that, he's not seriously injured, right?"

Erick shrugs. "He's a big boy. I'm sure he'll be fine." His tone carries less bravado than his words.

He turns down the alley and stops by the heavy metal side door leading into the Bell, Book & Candle. "Breakfast tomorrow morning? At Myrtle's Diner?"

I twist in my seat and stare. "Always, but don't you want to come in or something?" There's honestly not much I can offer him in my mini-fridge and microwave-equipped back room, and I'm not feeling brave enough to directly invite him up to my swanky apartment.

"Nah. Thanks, though."

My disappointment must be more obvious than I intend.

He reaches over and clasps my hand. "It's not that I wouldn't enjoy a nightcap, Moon. I've got a lot on my mind. I'm gonna head out to the icehouse on the lake and fish a little before I call it a night. I'll see you at breakfast." He leans over the center console and gives me a quick peck on the cheek.

"Yeah, sure. It was a big night. I'll see you in the morning." I jump out of the cruiser before I can say or do anything to embarrass myself.

He politely waits while I fish my keys out of my

coat pocket and fumble with the lock. Once I'm inside and the door has closed behind me, the sound of his engine fades as he backs down the alley and drives away.

Note to self: work on flirt game.

"Oh, I'm sure it's not you, dear."

"Grams! The rules! If these lips aren't moving, you don't get to comment. Stay out of my head, woman!" Maybe I'm overreacting, but my heart is racing and my bladder is quaking.

The late Myrtle Isadora smooths her silk-and-tulle Marchesa gown with one bejeweled hand, while she checks her manicure and ignores my reminder.

To be clear, my recently deceased grandmother didn't actually cross over. Her ghost is permanently tethered to this bookshop that she left me in her will.

"All rules aside, dear. You know how Erick feels about you. I'm sure there's some other reason he couldn't come in for a nightcap." Her ethereal hand rubs my back, and I find a strange otherworldly comfort in the gesture.

Arching an eyebrow teasingly, I offer my hypothesis. "One reason might be that I can't offer him an actual 'nightcap' since you won't allow me to store booze on the premises."

"Alcoholism is no joke, Mizithra." She clutches one of her strands of pearls and scowls.

"I know, Grams. One day at a time . . . and all that. I respect your struggle, but now that you're a ghost, shouldn't I be allowed to have a bottle of wine or two on standby?" I bat my eyelashes and my big grey eyes beg for leniency.

In true diva fashion, she ignores my question. "How was broomball?"

I bring her up to speed on the crowds, the co-coa, and the fights. "I better hit the hay. I have to be up, and functional, at an unmentionable hour to meet Erick for breakfast. I should've offered to bring him midmorning donuts instead."

"Sweet dreams, dear." She snickers as she fades through the wall into the printing museum.

She doesn't need to read my mind to know what I'm hoping to find in dreamland . . .

CHAPTER 2

THE STIFF BLACK hairs of my semi-wild caracal's tufted ears tickle my nose. "Really, Pyewacket? Was it absolutely necessary for you to wake me up five minutes before my alarm?"

"RE-ow." Feed me.

"Yes, Mr. Cuddlekins, your *command* is my command." I dig myself out from under the luxurious down comforter and search for my slippers. Reindeer onesie pajamas are all fine and good, but I won't last long with bare feet in this weather. An Arizona girl like me is used to high temperatures and dry air, and the brutal winters in almost-Canada are still a bit beyond my comfort zone.

Stumbling toward the plaster medallion that opens the secret door from my apartment, I trip over my fiendish feline, and narrowly escape a fall. "Pye, if you want me to serve up your Fruity Puffs, then at least clear a path for me to make it downstairs in one piece."

He calmly ceases his twisting around my legs and waits patiently while the door slides open. His understanding of the English language is impressive, and my grasp of the subtleties of *caracal* continues to improve.

The early morning light lacks the strength to penetrate the depths of the bookstore. Shadows linger in the curves and corners. As I trudge across the Rare Books Loft, a strange unease settles on my shoulders. Stopping halfway to the wrought-iron spiral staircase, I slowly turn and survey the neat rows of oak reading tables. None of the green-glass lampshades are aglow, and when I reach out with my extra senses, I don't feel anything suspicious.

"Maybe I still have one foot in dreamland, Pyewacket. You'd let me know if there was an intruder, right?"

"Reow." Can confirm.

I'm still figuring out what it means to be a psychic, and I don't always interpret the messages correctly. The magicked mood ring my grandmother left me is somehow responsible for triggering my latent abilities. However, as mood rings go, it's exceptionally cantankerous. The swirling mists within the black cabochon can be quite helpful, but only when they choose to be.

At the bottom of the winding staircase, I risk stepping over the "No Admittance" chain. Thankfully, the universe is smiling down on me today, and I manage to make it to the other side without tripping and falling.

Once I've squared away Pyewacket with a generous portion of his favorite sugary cereal, I brew myself some wake-up juice. As the welcome scent of java fills the back room, I reflect on my new bookfilled world.

One thing I don't miss about my life below the poverty line in the Southwest is working as a barista. Don't get me wrong, I love coffee. I can't imagine starting my day without a proper cup of black gold, but I prefer to order it at the diner, which is named after my grandmother and run by her first ex-husband. This little sip of go-go juice is designed to keep me from climbing back into bed and skipping my breakfast appointment with Erick.

I trudge upstairs with my cup of coffee and dress with my eyes half closed. Ghost-ma's absence is surprising, but I've barely got enough time to run down the block to the diner as it is. I'll search for her in the adjacent printing museum when I return.

The lessons I learned the hard way during my first winter, on the shores of the great lake that graces this region, have served me well. I've layered my clothing, tucked my scarf inside my jacket, and pulled my stocking hat down over my ears. My thick mittens make it impossible to send Erick a text, so I jog to stave off hypothermia and hope to arrive before I'm officially late.

I push open the door of Myrtle's Diner, and the smell of breakfast embraces me as I stomp my feet back to life and wave to my surrogate grandfather.

He peeks through the red-Formica-trimmed orders-up window and gives me his usual spatula salute.

Walking toward the corner booth, I'm surprised to see it empty. I slide onto the far bench so I can see the door and wave to Erick when he comes in. Although it hardly seems necessary, since the sole occupants of the restaurant are two locals at the counter and me.

My favorite waitress, Tally, slides a steaming mug of java onto the table along with a small melamine bowl of individual creamers. "Mornin', Mitzy. Did you hear about the storm?"

Since moving as far north as I have ever ventured in my life, I've learned that the hot topic of conversation in the winter is always the next storm. "I hear it might be worse than the blizzard in '84."

Tally puts a hand to her aproned chest and gasps. "You don't say? Well, I better run to the Piggly Wiggly after work and stock up on canned goods."

I nod and smile. I don't have the heart to tell her I was joking and actually have no knowledge of the legendary snowstorm of 1984.

After several satisfying sips of my coffee, my girlfriend senses and my extrasensory perceptions join forces. Something is definitely not right. First of all, Erick is never late. However, if he was going to be unavoidably late, he would absolutely text me.

Fishing my phone out of the large pocket of my puffy coat, I double check to make sure I didn't miss a message.

Nothing.

Odell strides out of the kitchen and places my breakfast in front of me. "Somethin' wrong?"

I drag my eyes away from the phone and stare at him for a moment. The grey utilitarian buzz cut speaks of practicality, and the deep lines of his face hold a lifetime of stories.

"I was supposed to meet Erick. It's not like him to be late."

He nods. "Not like him at all. You get started on your breakfast. I'm sure he'll walk through that door before you finish."

Our eyes meet, and I grin. "Um, have you met me?"

His coarse laughter warms my heart. "Ya got a point." Odell raps his knuckles twice on the silver-flecked table and returns to the kitchen.

Halfway through my scrambled eggs and chorizo, the mood ring on my left hand shudders with an icy warning.

Gazing down, the face of Deputy Paulsen stares back from the swirling cabochon.

Now, that's one way to ruin my appetite. I pick at the perfect, sacred home fries, which would normally be scarfed down without hesitation, and push my plate away.

Taking a last, desperate glug of coffee, I collect my dishes and tuck them in the bus bin behind the counter. Old habits die hard.

Waving goodbye to Odell and Tally, I slip my mittens back on and continue down Main Street to the sheriff's station.

Deputy Baird is manning the desk and, true to form, she's deeply involved in a game on her phone.

She barely looks up when I walk in, but nods her head anyway.

That is the official signal, which allows me unescorted access to Erick's office.

I push through the crooked wooden gate, inhale

the scent of burned coffee, and walk across the empty bullpen. As I approach the sheriff's office, a knot of resentment forms in my stomach. Based on Furious Monkeys' head nod, Erick is sitting at his desk. Why didn't he text me?

I'm working up a wronged-girlfriend speech as I turn the corner into his office. Imagine my surprise, and immense disappointment, when I discover Deputy Paulsen occupying his chair.

Caught off guard by her unwelcome presence, I blurt the first thing that pops into my head. "Erick isn't in here."

The portly deputy makes a show of searching under several stacks of papers on the desk and inside her coffee mug. "Nope. Not in here."

I shake off her reply. "Obviously. Let me rephrase my question, Deputy. Where is Sheriff Harper?"

She leans back in Erick's chair and fixes me with a self-satisfied grin as she jerks a thumb over her left shoulder. "Back in the holding cells."

I openly roll my eyes as I offer an insincere thanks and head down the narrow hallway. You may wonder how I know my way to the holding cells? Let's say that I've been there before, not as a visitor, and leave it at that.

Why was Paulsen looking so smug? She's probably soaking up the glory of sitting in the sheriff's chair. Ever since he defeated her in the last election, I've questioned her loyalties. Erick is always the first to say what a good cop she is, but one has to wonder. I push through the metal door at the end of the hallway and search the small passageway.

Maybe she was gleeful about sending me on a fool's errand. I definitely don't see Erick standing outside any of the cells. Maybe he's checking on a prisoner. "Sheriff Harper? Sheriff, are you back here?"

The hairs on the back of my neck lift in warning and I swear there's a soft groan.

Sounds like someone in pain. What if he's hurt?

Racing down the short drab corridor, I skitter to a stop in front of the middle holding cell. "Erick? What are you doing in there?"

My normally freshly scrubbed and shaved boyfriend is camped on the cold metal bench, head in hands, with a hint of stubble peppering his jaw. "I wish I could say I was glad to see you, Moon. I'm sorry I didn't call to cancel breakfast—they took my phone."

I grip the grey steel bars with both hands and pull my face close to the cell. "Who took your phone? What's going on? You're not making any sense."

He leans back against the cinderblock wall, and that's when I notice that there's no badge pinned on his uniform. The two empty eyelets shout a deadly warning.

My extrasensory perception offers a single clairaudient clue. "Murder." Suddenly, this morning's flash of uneasiness makes perfect sense. "Who was murdered?"

Erick's weary blue-grey eyes snap to attention. "Did Paulsen fill you in?"

I throw my arms up in the air. "No! No one is filling me in, including you. Would someone please tell me what's going on?"

"Gerhardt Klang's body was discovered outside the service entrance behind the ice rink this morning. The Zamboni driver comes in early to prepare the ice before the figure-skating lessons. He didn't recognize the victim. But when Paulsen and I arrived on the scene, and I realized who it was, I had to take myself off the case." His monotone voice belies the storm brewing beneath the surface.

"All right. You recused yourself. That kind of makes sense, but why are you sitting in a jail cell without your badge?"

"A lot of people saw the two of us fighting last night. They also heard me threaten the victim." Erick runs a hand through his hair and attempts to scrape the long bangs from his eyes. "Once Paulsen confirmed the ID of the victim and the deputies found my bloody jersey in the laundry bin, she asked me to surrender my badge and gun. She's holding me for questioning until she gets the ME's report."

I kick the bars with the toe of my snow boot and grimace at the unexpected pain. "Classic Paulsen, always overreacting and eager to arrest everyone. You're the sheriff. Can't you pardon yourself or something?"

Erick sighs heavily and slowly gets to his feet. He walks to the bars and reaches one hand through.

I slide my hand in his and get an immediate clairsentient dose of his uncertainty. "Hey, we both know you didn't do this. You're not a murderer. I'll look into things. You said it before, my hunches can be surprisingly accurate. I'll figure out who actually murdered Klang, and you'll be out of here in no time."

He squeezes my hand. "Thanks for believing in me. I don't think Paulsen honestly suspects me, but the evidence isn't in my favor right now. It's not a good idea for me to be seen poking around this case. I don't want any rumors of impropriety. It's probably for the best if I stay in here until someone clears me."

"Don't worry, *someone* will do exactly that.

Mitzy Moon is on the case." At least my grand-standing brings a weak smile to his lips.

I pull him closer and kiss him through the bars. "I'll bring you some lunch."

He stares at me with admiration. "Thanks, Moon."

CHAPTER 3

DURING THE BRISK walk back to the bookshop, I risk removing a mitten to place a call to my attorney, who also happens to be a powerful alchemist. I put the call on speaker and get my glove back on before frostbite claims a digit. "Good morning, Mr. Willoughby."

His sigh offers no indication of whether I've met his standards of etiquette. "Good morning, Mizithra. What is it you require?"

Busted. Although, I can't imagine why it offends him that my calls tend to coincide with when I need something. He should feel proud that I trust him so completely that it never occurs to me that he might not be able to help. However, his tone indicates he doesn't see it that way. "Silas, I'm sorry to bother you, but Erick is somehow in jail for the murder of some broomball player named Gerhardt Klang. Paulsen is having a field day holding him for questioning, but you and I both know there's no way he did this."

"Certainly not." Silas harrumphs. "Gerhardt Klang is an archeologist of considerable notoriety and a tenured professor in the anthropology department at the local community college. I was not aware he played sport. What evidence places your sheriff under suspicion?"

"All circumstantial. Erick got in a fight with the guy at the broomball game last night, and, in the heat of the moment, he kind of made some threatening statements." I swallow and add an afterthought. "Oh, and there was blood on Erick's game jersey, but that had to be from the fight."

Silas grumbles on the other end of the phone.

"What is it? That didn't sound like a good grumble."

"A powerful motive carries a degree of heft. I assume you'll be wanting a copy of the medical examiner's report."

"You couldn't be more correct, Mr. Willoughby."

"Very well. I will officially offer my services to Mr. Harper, and, acting on his behalf, obtain a copy of the ME's report as soon as it becomes available. Is that satisfactory?"

"That's completely awesome. I'll dig into this case and see what else I can find out. Any idea why Klang would play for Koochiching county's broomball team even though he was a professor at Birch County Community College?"

"I am afraid I do not follow the ins and outs of the Great White North's broomball league. I believe your best resource on that subject will be Twiggy."

"Copy that. Keep me posted, Silas."

"Indeed."

Ending the call with my mentor, I take a quick detour into the cul-de-sac on Main Street, beside the bookstore. The cold came early, but the snow is late. This combination allows for the formation of impossible ice walls and waves along the shore of our great lake.

Some of the fins and swirls are almost transparent, while others hold the whites of glacial milk. My desert-based childhood never prepared me for such a deep attraction to the cycles of water—the beauty of floes. It would've been amazing to visit this place with my mother. The tragedy of losing her when I was eleven hurts as freshly as if it were yesterday.

Wandering down memory lane causes me to lose track of time. Only the chill threatening to nip off my nose ends my reverie and turns me away from the harbor.

The thick wooden door at the front of my book-shop, with its intricate carvings of magical vignettes, is unlocked.

Twiggy is in the house.

Hurrying to the back room, I find her hunched over the keyboard of our ancient computer.

"Are you working on the weekly order?"

Her fingers abruptly stop and the chair sweeps around to reveal the irritated face of my volunteer employee. "Is that your idea of a joke, Your Highness?"

Oops. Time to do some serious backpedaling. "Not at all. I was legitimately asking. If it's not too much trouble, I need another skein of green yarn for the murder wall. You know we can't have red, because it reminds Grams of blood and gives her a fright. I don't want to be accused of scaring any ghosts."

This jab at my grandmother brings a chuckle, and Twiggy nods her head appreciatively. "I wish I could see her, you know. You and Silas are lucky. You got the gift, and he's got those transmuted spectacles he's always bragging about. You say her ghost looks about thirty-five, eh? She was in her sixties when she passed, and, of course, she'd been sick for a couple years . . . Sure would be nice to see her looking young and full of life."

This unusually verbose speech from Twiggy

catches me off guard and I nearly forget what I came for. "Yeah, I wish you could see her too. She looks great in that fancy dress, with all her rings and strands of pearls."

Twiggy shakes off her brief foray into emotions like a dog drying his coat after a dash into the lake. "Anyway, you musta wanted something before I went on a trot down flashback drive. What can I do ya for?"

Her folksy twist brings a smile despite my agitated state. "Gerhardt Klang was murdered last night. I'm—"

"Boy, oh boy! Good thing Harper's got a badge. If not, he'd be my number one suspect." Twiggy cackles and slaps her thigh.

The color drains from my face and I struggle to find the right words.

Her eyes widen. "You can't be serious? That devil of a deputy! How could she think for one minute—?"

"Well, she does. Erick is sitting in a holding cell right now waiting for a time-of-death ruling from the medical examiner. I need to dig into this, Twiggy. Everyone's always saying that Paulsen is a good cop, but we both know she's had her eyes on the sheriff's chair for quite a while."

"I'm your gal. Erick's the best lawman this town has had in decades. What do you need?"

"I probably need to know more about the victim. If I can understand him, hopefully I can figure out who else had a motive. I mean, who has *the* motive."

Twiggy leans back in the cracked, brown-leather office chair and crosses her arms. "Shoot."

"All right, first off, why did Klang play for the Koochiching Arctic Arrows if he was a professor at BCCC?"

Twiggy lets out a low whistle. "That is not a short story, doll."

Pulling out a weather-beaten wooden chair from under the small table, I take a seat and match her pose. "I've got nothing but time."

By the time Twiggy finishes breaking down the finer points of the various rivalries and secret alliances amongst the teams, I'm shocked to still be awake.

"So, to shorthand it, Klang is an arrogant so-and-so, and only wanted to play for a team that he could captain?"

She nods curtly. "That's the gist of it."

"What do you know about his day job?"

Twiggy sniffs and shrugs. "Not a thing."

"Great. How am I going to find out why a bigwig professor, in the prime of his life, is teaching at a community college in almost-Canada?"

Twiggy shivers uncontrollably. "Isadora? Is that you?"

Grams pops into the visible spectrum with a mischievous grin. "Tell Twiggy it's me, and everything's fine, and then—I have an idea!"

Tilting my head toward Twiggy, I confirm her suspicions. "What's your idea, Grams?"

She rubs her ethereal hands together gleefully. "You could go undercover at the community college!" She shrieks with glee, throws her hands in the air, and spins like a dervish.

"Grams thinks I should go undercover as a BCCC student."

Twiggy groans and shakes her head. "Let's agree amongst ourselves to call it 'the college.' It's the only one around; not like there'll be a lot of confusion."

"Understood. What do you think about her plan?"

"Might as well. I'll work my contacts in the broomball league and you can make nice with some students."

My shoulders droop and I flop forward, banging my forehead on the table. "The things we do for love. I didn't enjoy college the first time around. Hooray for second chances."

Grams swirls around the room, spouting off addendums to her astonishing plan. "I'm sure you can use the same name you used before, Darcy something. Technically, you never went to the college even though you were posing as a college student . . . but that was at the high school. Never mind. The name's fine. I'll start working on wardrobe. You'll have to get Silas to mockup some identity papers. You're starting right before Thanksgiving break, and you'll need to have transfer paperwork or something."

"*Mamma Mia!*, Grams. Simmer down. I'm pretty sure this is one of those situations that can be easily handled by a large donation. And, if it happens to go to the anthropology or archaeology department, it seems like that might make the perfect *in.*"

Twiggy stands and rakes a hand through her short grey hair. "They'll need a temporary professor."

"Silas!" The three of us shout in unison.

Grams works on wardrobe and backstory, while I make a quick phone call to Mr. Willoughby to confirm that he has the necessary background to teach the archaeology classes while the community college searches for a replacement for Professor Klang. Was there ever any doubt? He also has an idea how to grease the wheels for my late-semester enrollment.

I reach up to pull the candle sconce lever,

which activates the sliding bookcase door to my secret apartment, and smile. If anyone had grabbed this heartbroken kid as she was bouncing from one foster home to another and told her what the future would be like, she probably would've punched him in the nose and called him a dirty liar.

I stride across the thick Persian carpets in my beautiful apartment toward the walk-in home for a collection of vintage clothing—a place I like to call wall-to-wall *Sex and the City* meets *Confessions of a Shopaholic*—and whisper, "Progress looks good on me."

"What's that, dear?"

"Nothing. Wondering what you plan on forcing me to wear, and whether or not we can negotiate a heel in the two-inch range?"

Grams giggles mercilessly. "If you want access to the best gossip, you gotta have something other people want. And everybody wants designer handbags and Jimmy Choos."

"I'm sorry I asked."

"Nonsense. Let's go with the blonde-to-russet ombré wig, the distressed designer jeans, with Jimmy Choo boots and this Mark Jacobs satchel. You can pretend it's a book bag."

"Yes, Mistress."

Her ability to affect matter at will is nonstop now. She's grabbing clothes and shoes from their resting places, tossing them wildly onto the padded mahogany bench in the center of the walk-in closet.

I wiggle my toes into the carpet, dreading a full day in high heels. "Can't I be the cool geeky kid who wears skinny jeans, high-tops, and ironic snarky T-shirts that say things like 'Wanted: Dead & Alive—Schrödinger's Cat'?"

Grams freeze frames and her image flickers like an old VHS tape.

"Grams? What is it?"

"Mizithra Achelois Moon, I did not break my promise to your father, and spend the last months of my life filling this closet for you, to have you simply toss it all aside for *skinny jeans*."

"Sorry, Grams." However, her comment gets me thinking. "I'm going to run across the alley and check on Dad. He was supposed to get back from the railroad convention in New York two days ago, but I haven't heard from him." I slowly back out of the closet.

"You'll be trying all of this on as soon as you get back, sweetie."

"Yes, Mistress."

Her tinkling laughter echoes off the tin-plated ceiling as I make a hasty retreat.

CHAPTER 4

THE DUNCAN RESTORATIVE JUSTICE FOUNDATION is open for business and the kind young woman seated in the reception area is either guessing, based on the bone-white hair my father and I share, or she has a reference photo of me next to her computer.

I'm sure I've never met her before, but as I stride across the terrazzo floor, temporarily distracted by the life-size bronze of my grandfather, Cal Duncan, she calls out a greeting.

"Hello, Mitzy. Your father is in the penthouse. Would you like me to announce you?"

"Sure. Also, I forgot my passkey."

She smiles politely, but her eyes are flecked with suspicion.

Definitely as sharp as she looks. I don't actually

have a passkey. It's not that I asked for one and my father refused; it never occurred to me to ask.

"No problem, Miss Moon. I'll program the elevator to take you to the penthouse floor."

"Wow! Hi-tech. Thanks."

I enter the marble-clad hallway and step into the plush elevator. Everything is so shiny and new, even the buttons have a posh glow.

The melodic ding of the bell precedes the door sliding open to reveal the towering figure of my father. "Mitzy! I've been so busy since I got back. Sorry I didn't call."

"No problem."

He wraps his powerful arms around me and kisses the top of my head, as I close my eyes and grin from ear to ear. I'm still getting used to the idea of having a dad. So far, I like it.

Amaryllis walks out of the back room with her hair in a haphazard bun, wearing a thick bathrobe and fuzzy unicorn slippers. A hint of camphor and eucalyptus wafts down the hall. "Don't come any closer. I caught a nasty cold while we were in New York and I definitely don't want you to get it. So, I'll say hello and goodbye from a distance and let you and your dad catch up."

"Thanks for the warning. And I love your slippers."

She chuckles, which causes her to launch into a

coughing fit, waves goodbye and shuffles back into the bedroom.

Dad and I walk into the kitchen and he motions for me to grab a seat at the breakfast bar while he brews us some coffee.

"So things must be pretty great with you and Amaryllis if she's comfortable being sick around you?"

Jacob's broad shoulders shake with laughter. "Yeah, things are wonderful. She was a real trooper in New York. She loaded up on decongestants and coffee to get through our meetings, but by the time our plane touched down in Pin Cherry, she was ready to collapse. I've been catching up on emails and playing nursemaid for the last couple days, but she deserves it."

He sets my coffee on the polished black granite counter and places one hand on his refrigerator door. "Cream alone, right?"

"You know me so well."

We share a chuckle, and he nods. "I'm getting better. I remember our first lunch, when I attempted to share your french fries."

"Rookie mistake, Duncan."

He laughs and passes me the creamer. "So, what's new in Pin Cherry?"

Pouring a little milky goodness into my java, I

watch it swirl. "Unfortunately, Erick is sitting in a jail cell suspected of murder."

"What? Sheriff Harper is a suspect?" My father tilts his head in disbelief.

I quickly explain the details of the situation and the unfortunate broomball fight.

Jacob's expression turns serious. "Broomball is no joke around here. The rivalries are brutal."

"Did you play?"

He nods and takes a deep breath. "I played intramural in college, but I preferred the speed and violence of hockey when I was a kid."

I arch one eyebrow. "Well, good news. Broomball has significantly upped its violence quotient."

"So what's your angle on this case?"

"Hmmm? What makes you think I have a case?"

His head drops and lolls from side to side. "Come on, Mitzy. I may be new to this dad thing, but I know enough to be certain you've got a plan to clear Erick's name."

"All right. Ya got me. I'm going undercover as an archaeology student at the college. Silas will be the temporary replacement professor, so between the two of us, we should be able to uncover some additional suspects."

"Sounds like a pretty good plan. Let me know if there's anything I can do."

"Thanks, Dad. I will. However, I have to get back. Grams—" My eyes widen and I lower my voice to a whisper. "Does she know about Grams?" I point meaningfully to the bedroom. "And me seeing ghosts and stuff?"

My father shakes his head. "It doesn't come up naturally, you know?"

My thoughts immediately turn to Erick. "I know better than you think. Anyway, I have to get back and endure a wardrobe session with, *you know who*."

His smile is everything. "Trust me, I have many reasons to be happy that I was born a *son* and not a daughter."

I chuckle knowingly as I step into the elevator.

"Oh, Mitzy, do you have plans for Thanksgiving?"

I've never actually had plans for Thanksgiving in my entire life. I shrug, and as the doors slide closed, I reply, "I don't think so."

My stomach tingles as the elevator drops. Plans for Thanksgiving? I never imagined myself thinking about something so domestic. I certainly won't be hosting anything at the bookshop. A mini-fridge and a microwave don't scream gourmet kitchen. Maybe I should ask around?

Passing through the lobby, I give a friendly wave to the receptionist.

In an effort to postpone my appointment with fashion destiny . . . I believe this community college student needs to do some back-to-school shopping!

The phrase ignites a series of sweet childhood memories. Before my mother was killed, and I became a perpetual foster child, August was our traditional spree. Cora Moon was a fiercely independent single mother, forsaken by her family, but determined to raise her daughter with every advantage. She would save whatever she could from the two or three jobs she was juggling, and we would spend a whole evening planning out our route.

At the time, I had no idea that shopping at second-hand stores could be frowned upon by certain segments of society. I felt like a princess. On one glorious Saturday in August, we would make our way to anywhere from five to ten second-hand stores and thrift shops in our search for clothes, shoes, and the occasional amazing backpack. I always felt so special. I had a mountain of new clothes and an entire day of my mother's time, which was the best part. I didn't understand how precious it truly was.

Once I entered the foster system, school shopping became a distant memory. I had my handful of well-worn items, and, possibly, if I had severely outgrown them, I would be allowed to purchase something new. Generally, I received hand-me-downs from the biological children or older foster children in the same home.

Cut to—

Grams severely over-indulging my clothing needs with a designer dream closet.

A quick trip over to Rex's Drugs for a notebook or two seems to be in order. I wave through the window of the diner as I hurry past, coat zipped tightly against the weather.

The bell dings when I enter the drugstore, and an elderly woman with a beautiful mountain of snow-white hair piled atop her head offers a friendly wave. "Welcome to Rex's. I'm the missus. Rex passed away several years ago." Her warm smile continues to beam, and she pats her carefully pinned beehive. "You and I have the same stylist." She laughs and slaps her hand on the counter.

My time in this small, friendly town has changed me. A year ago, I would've thrown a fake smile her way and dove between the aisles without a word. However, I've grown accustomed to this slower pace of life and learned firsthand the benefit of friends. "Were you born a snow princess like me, or did you have to earn it?" This comment brings uproarious laughter from Mrs. "Rex."

"Oh my, you are as sharp as everyone says. Of course, you must be Mitzy Moon. Not a lot of folks with that hair and those hips in this town."

My smile wavers as I consider the "hips" compliment. Backhanded compliment or folksy banter? Not that it matters. I'm not operating under the mistaken impression that I resemble a string bean. "That's me. I'm actually here for some stationery supplies. Where are your pens and notebooks?"

She points with her left hand. "You'll find all that stuff in aisle three. And if you don't mind a seasonal theme, there are some sheets of spring-flower paper on sale."

"Thank you kindly." I meander down aisle three and peruse the selection. Since I'm not an actual student, I don't actually need *anything*. But she's sweet, and I'm sure Twiggy will figure out what to do with whatever I buy. I grab three notebooks, two packs of ink pens, a roll of tape, and a handful of spring-themed sheets. On my way to the counter, I notice a little rack of books. Maybe Erick would like some reading material. The fact that I own a three-story bookshop, bursting at the seams with volumes, does not prevent me from buying the latest best-selling mystery novel for my incarcerated boyfriend.

"I'm glad to see you picked up some of the spring paper. It's a great price and you really can use it year 'round." She rings up the sheets and slips them into a bag. "Well, these pens are very nice. Blue and black. That's such a good idea. You know they're erasable?" She slips the pens into the bag.

"Oh, they're erasable. That's good." I suppress an eye roll.

"You know, I think this tape is buy one, get one at fifty percent off, if you want to grab another roll."

I don't feel like I have the option to say no. "Oh, great. I'll go grab another one right now."

She waits patiently for me to return with the second roll of tape. She doesn't ring up a single thing in my absence.

"So that's one full price and a second roll at fifty percent off." She taps in the price of the two rolls of tape—longhand—and adds them to the bag. "You'll love these notebooks. The pages tear out smooth, so you don't have all those little fidgety bits all over your nice carpet."

I nod and smile.

"Oh, I've heard good things about this book. You must read a lot of mysteries, with all the sleuthing that you do."

Dear Lord baby Jesus! Does this woman know everything there is to know about me? And is she going to finish this transaction anytime this century? "It's for a friend."

She leans across the counter and lowers her voice to a conspiratorial whisper. "I heard about Sheriff Harper being in the clink. I tell you what, I've known that boy since he was knee-high to a grasshopper, and he wouldn't hurt a fly! The thought." She shakes her head in dismay.

I clench my teeth and double-down on the smile. At long last, the purchase process comes to a close. I hand her my cash, because cash is king in Pin Cherry. Almost no one takes credit or debit cards. I've learned that the hard way.

"Well, you let Erick know we're all pulling for him, sweetie."

"I sure will. Thank you so much."

The frosty air waiting for me outside is a welcome cool down. Clearer heads and all.

I'm suddenly struck by the urgent need to visit Erick and update him on my plans. Plus, I promised him some lunch. I better run and place my order before the rush hits.

When I pop into Myrtle's Diner, Odell already has an order of meatloaf and mashed potatoes packaged to go.

"Thanks, mind reader."

He smiles briefly. "Anytime." His expression hardens and he shakes his head. "You let him know, we're all pullin' for him."

Nodding, I beat a silent retreat.

No one questions my return to the station, so I head to the cells without hesitation. The color of the walls seems as though it was chosen specifically to drain one's will to live.

Erick's stubble is a little scruffier and his mood has definitely soured.

"Hey, I thought I'd stop by with your lunch and give you an update."

He nods. "There isn't one."

I maneuver his takeout through the bars and set the trade paperback on top.

He doesn't budge.

"It's meatloaf from the diner, and I got you some reading material. Also, I'm supposed to let you know they're all pulling for you." I withdraw my hand and offer a weak smile. "There might not technically be an update on the autopsy, but Silas has agreed to represent you and I'm going undercover at the community college to see if I can find any additional suspects."

Erick is too exhausted to muster appreciation.

I happen to know firsthand how frustrating it is to be accused of a crime you didn't commit, but I'm a little surprised he's so depressed. "Erick, why are you letting this get to you? You're the sheriff. You're on the right side of the law. You know how this works. We get the medical examiner's report, we confirm the time of death, and your alibi takes you off the list. You're in the clear, and Paulsen will be forced to do some actual investigating and find another suspect."

He leans against the bland beige bricks and the muscles in his jaw flex with tension. "It's not gonna be that easy, Moon."

"Why not? Of course it will be that easy."

"I don't have an alibi."

"What? I'm sure your mom heard you come home last night, right?"

His silence is unsettling.

Quick side note: he bought his mom a house when he got back from his second tour in Afghanistan to repay her for all her years of hard work as a single parent, making sacrifices to raise him right. Now he lives with her and takes care of her. It's extremely sweet and seems like a built-in alibi. I'm confused by his lack of faith in his mother's hearing. "Erick, what aren't you telling me? You dropped me off, and then what?"

"I went out to the icehouse to fish. I was upset about the fight with Klang, and knew I wouldn't be able to sleep. I lost track of time. There was a bottle of bourbon in the ice chest. Long story short, I didn't think I should drive home."

"You slept in the icehouse?"

"I slept in the icehouse. I had barely pulled into the driveway this morning when I got the call about a body at the rink. I ran inside the house, changed into my uniform, and wound up in this cell. So—"

"So, no matter what time Klang was murdered, you'll still be a suspect." I grip the bars and let my head rest against the cool metal tubing. "I can be your alibi."

He looks at me as though the distance across that small cell is a vast ocean. His eyes are a mix of gratitude and disappointment. "I would never ask you to lie for me, Moon. I appreciate the offer. I do. But I didn't kill him, and there's gotta be another way to prove that."

"Silas and I will find something. You know me. I never give up."

At least my words bring the hint of a smile to his strong jaw. "Yeah, I know. I'm also curious to see your disguise."

For the first time since he landed in the cell, there's a tiny spark of life in his eyes.

"No problem, Sheriff. Darcy Brown starts school tomorrow. If you're still in here, I'm sure she can bring you some dinner." My efforts finally pay off and he enjoys a hearty laugh at my expense.

"Looking forward to it." He locates the motivation to take two strides and retrieve his meal.

My heart hurts for him.

He picks up the sack and leans to meet me through the bars. "Thanks, Moon."

Our lips meet in a forlorn excuse for a kiss.

"You know, I always did like a bad boy, Harper."

My lame attempt at humor barely rates a half grin. The flash of levity vanishes and the weight of his situation once again settles over him.

Deflated, I turn to leave. "See ya tomorrow, Sheriff."

The crinkling of a paper sack is my only reply.

CHAPTER 5

My dreams, or rather nightmares, are filled with various unnerving possibilities for Klang's death. In each scenario, Erick plays the bloodthirsty murderer and Klang the helpless victim. I finally tear myself from the grip of my horrible imaginings and snuggle against the warmth of Pyewacket, curled up beside me.

In the faint glimmer of dawn's first light, Pye studies me with a look that says he senses my agitation. He pushes his broad head against my hand and purrs softly.

"Don't take this the wrong way, Pye, but if this is what is meant by 'for better or worse,' I'm not sure I'm cut out for it."

"Nonsense, dear."

My heart seizes up in my chest, and the fears from dreamland are suddenly palpable. "Grams, again, I beg you to use the slow, sparkly reentry. I haven't slept at all. I'm a nervous wreck. Plus, I feel super guilty because a teeny-tiny part of me almost believes Erick is guilty."

"That's perfectly natural, Mitzy. Deep down, you know that Erick didn't do this, but you saw another side of him at the broomball arena. Accepting all of him is a process."

"What if I can't do it? What if I'm only attracted to gorgeous, kindhearted, generous Erick? What if I can't accept his shadow side?"

"I wish I had the answers, sweetie. But let's not forget, I had five husbands and more than a handful of special friends. I'm not sure I ever stuck around long enough to get to know anyone's shadow side. The closest I ever got was probably with your grandpa Cal, but even then I cut bait before anything was truly resolved."

"Great. My lone source of relationship advice is from a serial short-term monogamist."

She exhales sharply. "You don't have to say it like it's such a bad thing. I do have a lot of experience with getting relationships off on the right foot."

"Hooray." I raise my arms in a weak, half-hearted cheer. "I might as well get up and do some investigating before class. There's no point lying here and imagining the worst."

Grams pumps her translucent fist in the air. "That's the spirit. Get out there and prove Erick's innocent."

Hardly able to muster the enthusiasm to change into my going out in public clothes, I can't begin to share Grams' excitement.

After bundling up against the freezing early morning temperatures, I pour my fur baby's breakfast and drive over to the arena.

There's already a truck in the parking lot, and when I try the back door, it's unlocked.

"Hello. Hello. Anyone here?"

The thrumming of an engine and an unpleasant scraping sound echo from the rink.

I thread my way through the back passageway and peer out of a doorway toward the ice. Not that I would know, but the enormous machine skimming across the ice like a polar lawnmower must be a Zamboni. The driver can't hear me, and I'm pleased to take the opportunity to snoop around unhindered.

There are two separate sets of locker rooms. One set appears to be public locker rooms for men and women, and the other is private locker rooms for the Abominables and the She-bominables. The guys' team got the better end of that naming scheme.

I try the door on the team's locker room and, since the handle turns, I take it as an invitation.

Inside the blue-and-gold shrine to the Abominables are the expected bank of lockers, each displaying a player's last name, but also a surprising number of amenities. A huge freezer filled with bagged blocks of ice and three stainless-steel whirlpools. Looks like they could be filled with either hot water or ice-bath therapies, based on the piping. I don't have a great deal of first-hand sporting experience, but I'm a walking Wikipedia of film and television. I've seen plenty of players forced to soak their aching joints in tubs filled with ice. I'm sure it helps, but it's definitely one more reason I have no interest in being a team player.

Each of the blue metal lockers is secured with a combination lock.

Except Harper's.

His lock is missing.

Noted.

A huge malodorous canvas cart with a metal frame and industrial-size wheels is solidly packed with used terrycloth towels and equally abused jerseys. I can't imagine the deputies took the time to stuff the dirty laundry down tight. That means that Erick's bloody jersey was right on top.

Also noted.

Moving on.

Other than the surprising cleanliness of the showers and the relatively mild stench in the rest of the locker room, there is nothing else to report.

As I step out of the changing room, the ominous silence is hard to miss.

Uh oh. Sounds like the Zamboni driver has finished, and without the guiding hum of the engine to pinpoint his location, my mind spins in search of a cover story as I return from whence I came.

One thing my vast media knowledge has taught me is that looking guilty and running are two of the worst possible ideas.

My casual stroll toward the back door is expectedly interrupted.

"Hey, what are you doing in here? The rink doesn't open until six."

"Oh, there you are. I heard the machine, and then I got all turned around. My little Billy is crazy about ice-skating, and one of the other moms told me this is the place to get lessons. Is there a sign-up sheet or a list of available coaches?"

Luckily, my ditzy mom routine works like a charm.

"Look, lady, I'm sure your little Billy is going to be the next Michelle Kwan. The rink opens at six. Students and coaches will be here at *six*."

How convenient that this crabby old cuss is

more concerned with making me feel stupid than determining my true purpose.

"Thank you so much! I will absolutely come back at six and see if I can get Billy signed up. Sure do appreciate the information. Have a wonderful day."

He grumbles under his breath as he turns toward the locker rooms.

Heading to the back door, I pause to inspect the lock.

One of my foster brothers taught me more than any girl should know about picking locks, and this one isn't particularly difficult. However, the person who forced their way into the arena didn't bother using a lock pick and tension wrench. The strike plate shows clear signs of forced entry. Seems like something even Paulson would've noticed.

I cannot wait to get my hands on those reports.

Back at amateur sleuth headquarters, Ghost-ma is swirling frantically around the apartment. She's pushed the rolling corkboard we affectionately call the murder wall into the middle of the room and she's had the audacity to make a card for Erick.

"Myrtle Isadora Johnson Linder Duncan Willamet Rogers! How dare you accuse my boyfriend of murder!"

"Listen, dear, you're the one who taught me how the murder wall works. For now, he's a suspect.

He absolutely has a connection to the victim. It's your job to find the actual killer and clear Erick's name. My job is to put the cards on the board."

"Oh brother." I stomp into the closet, peel off my wonderful comfy clothes, and strap in to the wardrobe of ace archaeology student, Darcy Brown.

"You really are becoming an expert with wigs, Mitzy. You got that thing in place and securely fastened with bobby pins before I even had a chance to offer suggestions."

Her praise brings a smile to my face. "I had an excellent teacher."

She presses her hand to her bounteous bosom and a little tear sparkles in the corner of her eye.

"Don't you dare start crying, Grams. You and Pyewacket hold the fort while I go shake down some community college students." I give my wig a little tug and fluff the ends. "I promised to take Erick his dinner after school, but when I get back we'll recap my first day. Wish me luck!"

"You won't need it, dear. Everyone's going to love you."

I cross my fingers and hope that her statement results from an afterlife clairvoyant message, rather than the inclinations of a love-is-blind grandmother.

The Birch County Community College is not what I expected. The underwhelming architecture consists of rows of square buildings around a central

greenbelt. However, the *quantity* of square buildings does not fail to impress.

Parking my Jeep in a visitor's space, I follow the
signs to the registrar. The week before Thanksgiving has taken its toll on staffing, and many of the
desks in the open-plan office area stand empty. I approach one of the service counters where a forlorn
student worker scrolls through her phone in an effort to stave off boredom.

"Excuse me. Hi, I'm Darcy Brown. Today's my
first day. Could you print out a schedule for me, or
something? I'm an archeology student, but I think
it's part of the Anthro Department here."

The girl's large brown eyes roll upward to meet
my gaze. She swallows and stares. Her lack of a
verbal response is perplexing.

I place a hand over my mouth, look around the
space, and double-check my info. "Am I in the
wrong department? Classic me. First day and I'm
already making an idiot of myself. Please point me
toward wherever I'm supposed to go, and I'll
vanish."

She blinks twice. "You're starting today? Next
week is Thanksgiving."

Yikes, I've captured a live one. "I know, right?
Leave it to me to pull up roots and transfer at the
weirdest possible time. It's totally the worst."

Something I said sparks her interest, and it appears I'll finally get the help I'm seeking. She leans toward me and lowers her voice. "I'm supposed to send people over to the kiosk, to print out their own schedules. But that stupid thing is always on the blink. I'll print one for you, real quick." Her fingers fly over the keyboard and, as the printer springs to life behind her, she finds even more words. "Oh, the anthropology department is in the science building, straight across the quad from us, and to your left two buildings. Do you want to buy your books before class? Some people like to buy them and try to impress the professors, and some people wait until after they get the syllabus. Do you know what you wanna do?"

"I have no idea. Like, I don't even know if I'll stay in this advanced class, or this town. I mean, my grades are good, but who's ever heard of Birch County?"

Her initial facial expression indicates I've offended her, but as her eyes take in my glorious hair and designer satchel, she changes her tact. "You don't have to tell me. This place has got to rank at the bottom of the list of best party schools, you know?"

I share one of my best fake giggles as she hands me my schedule.

She points to the class at the top of the list. "It looks like your lecture ends at 11:30. If you want to swing by, I can show you what to avoid at the cafeteria."

Taking the sheet of paper, I paste on a big smile. "Thanks. That's super nice. I have no idea how aggro my professors will be about me transferring so late. So, if I have, like, a mound of assignments, I may have to skip lunch. Thank you so much."

Slipping the useless schedule in my Marc Jacobs bag, my psychic senses confirm that the persona of Darcy Brown is working in my favor. Maybe Grams was right about the power of the bling!

After one wrong turn, I find the lecture hall where a "Mr. Willoughby" is taking roll.

He looks up as I enter and effortlessly masks any response.

While I attempt to descend the stairs as quietly as possible, in four-inch heels, the professor runs a finger down his roll sheet.

"Either you are Darcy Brown or Rebecca Jankowski."

Typical Silas. Even the simplest statement carries the threat of a trap.

I drop into the nearest empty seat and reply, "I'm Darcy Brown. I don't have my textbook yet, but if you have an extra syllabus, I'm sure I can pick it up this afternoon."

He harrumphs into his bushy grey mustache, and the fluorescent lighting bounces off his bald head as he peers up the stadium seating in my direction. "I think you'll find that in an advanced class, such as this, we will rely far more on field experience than texts." He selects a potsherd from a tray on the counter next to his podium and holds it up. "Who can tell me about this?"

An eager girl in the front row adjusts her messy updo and raises her hand.

Silas refers to something on his podium, most likely the roll sheet. "Yes, Miss Rey."

"That is a shard from an Anishinaabeg water vessel. Circa 1600s. The fragment displays the classic Anishinaabeg symbol for water." She leans back and smiles.

"Incorrect." He exhales and glances around the hall. "Miss Brown, please come down to the front."

Looks like I'm destined to be teacher's toy, rather than teacher's pet. My heels click down the steps, and three of the girls sitting in the front row, including Messy Bun, make no effort to hide their shoe envy.

"Hold out your hands, Miss Brown." The now familiar scents of pipe tobacco and denture cream accompany the command.

I do as I'm told, and Silas drops the broken bit of pottery into my palms. His milky eyes fix me with a meaningful stare. "What can *you* tell me, Miss Brown?"

Clearly, that simple phrase is code for, "Tap into your extrasensory perceptions, Mitzy." Time to impress the cool kids. I grip the shard in both hands, take a deep breath, and focus on the piece of history. "Yucatán Peninsula. 500 to 550 CE. Mayan. A ceremonial vessel used for blood offerings." The image that provided that last thread of information turns my stomach, and it's a genuine struggle to keep from dropping the sacred piece of history and running.

Professor Willoughby holds out his hand and I return the fragment.

Having had more than my share of experiences with Silas and his mysterious ways, I return to my seat without waiting for confirmation. This wreaks havoc on the calm disinterest of the front-row girls.

Messy Bun blurts, "Is that right? Is she right, Professor?"

Silas sets down the remnant and smooths his mustache with a thumb and forefinger. "Indeed. Algonquin pictographs tend to be syllabary, while Mayan glyphs are modular. Each hieroglyph contains several elements, as Miss Brown accurately deduced."

Messy Bun and her friends whisper and shoot me suspicious looks.

"She just got lucky. If I'd been able to hold it in my hands, I'm sure I would've been able to tell that the symbol wasn't Anishinaabeg. It really wasn't a fair test, Professor."

The subtle tilt of Mr. Willoughby's cranium tells me all I need to know. "Very well. Come forward."

Poor thing, she's in over her head.

Silas selects a piece with delicate carving, despite its heft, and a large green accent stone, and places it gently in her hands. "What can you tell me of this?"

She glances at her cohorts and gives a smug grin. "It's a Chinese carving. Liang Dynasty. 502 to 557 CE. Most likely a wedding gift. This elongated jade piece attached to the top is a fertility symbol." She hands the carving back to Silas.

"Incorrect. You may return to your seat."

Her eyelids twitch, and the rasp of her dry swallow reaches all the way up to the fifth row.

"Miss Brown, will you return?"

Once again I walk to the front of the room, and Silas places the carving in my hands.

An odd heat trickles up my arms and a series of ancient rites race through my head in a clairvoyant montage. "It is a form of jade, nephrite. However, it's known by the name greenstone, or pounamu in the Maori tongue. This item is a ceremonial adze. It's an item belonging to the chief, passed from father to son, marking rank and power in their society. This particular carving is from the time known as Classic Maori Material Culture, in New Zealand, 1400 to 1500 CE." The images of war and struggle tighten my throat and I'm unable to continue. I pass the powerful artifact back to its current caretaker.

The flood of information doesn't cease. Instead, as I grip the counter to steady myself, the words "deadly secret" throb in my skull. Unsure whether they're tied to the object I was reading for Silas or something else, I swallow uncomfortably and hurry back to my seat.

Messy Bun raises her hand.

Silas waves her hand away. "Miss Brown is correct on all counts. While the debate still rages over Polynesian versus Chinese influence on early Maori culture, this adze is a remarkable example of the carving style unique to the tribes of New Zealand."

He turns and writes three separate book titles on the whiteboard. "Take the last ten minutes of class to divide into three groups. Each group will present a critique on one of these volumes tomorrow."

Hands shoot up in the air, and whispers and grumbles spread across the lecture hall.

Silas picks up his tray of artifacts and exits through a back door.

The students, including me, are left staring at each other in speechless frustration.

Messy Bun and her two wing-women race up the steps toward my seat. "Darcy, do you want to be in our group?"

Back in the days of friendless foster care, my rules about protecting myself would've prevented accepting this offer. I would've tossed out a snarky response and marched out of the room, not much caring whether I had an assignment to turn in. But I'm here to prove my boyfriend's innocence, so I'll have to swallow my pride and pander to the lowest common denominator. Welcome to Mitzy 2.0!

I muster up some enthusiasm and reply, "Really? That's super sweet of you. Like, I don't know anyone, and I'm so worried about this project. I would totally love to be in your group. Thank you so much."

My two afternoon classes are entry-level science courses, and I don't bump into any of the students from the morning's advanced class.

No additional messages are delivered from the ether, and I make a firm decision to avoid these classes in the future. This way lies madness, and a dead end.

The road to information runs directly through Messy Bun and her cohorts. The best plan of attack is to lure them in with my fancy clothes, and then pump them for information while they're distracted by my accouterment. I have no idea if Klang's actual killer is associated with the college, but *this* archaeology student is definitely on a dig!

CHAPTER 6

BEFORE I MEET my super-awesome prehistory group at the dormitories, I barely have enough time to take Erick an early dinner.

There's no deputy at the desk when I enter the sheriff's station, and the overall feeling in the air is heavy and somber. So much so, that even someone without benefit of psychic perceptions could pick up on the negative energy. I head to the holding cells and am surprised to find Erick clean-shaven and in civilian clothes.

"What happened? Do I smell lavender? Was it prisoner makeover day?"

My tendency to use humor as a coping mechanism has the desired effect, and a weak smile flickers on his handsome face. "Not even Deputy Paulson can stop Gracie Harper."

"Are you saying that your mom was here? I thought she couldn't drive?"

"Oh, she can't. Her vision is atrocious." He shakes his head. "However, she went door-to-door in her neighborhood, make that *our* neighborhood, telling each and every one of the neighbors how I had been wrongly accused and was being held under horrible conditions, until one of them offered to drive her into town."

I hold up the paper sack containing a burger and fries and shrug. "Well, this makes my delivery seem pretty pathetic."

He strides across the cell and his hand lunges through the bars. "Is that a bacon cheeseburger? Please tell me that's a bacon cheeseburger."

"You know Odell would never disappoint you."

He eagerly takes the sack and mumbles several thank-yous under his breath as he returns to the metal bench seat to enjoy his meal.

"Silas left me a voicemail—"

Erick's assault on the french fries ceases. He looks at me and raises an eyebrow.

"Let me finish. He said the medical examiner had released her report but that I would probably want to talk to you about the findings."

He nods and picks up the pace of his chewing.

"Look, I'm not gonna spoil your dinner. Take

your time. Enjoy your delicious burger and let me tell you about my day."

He swallows loudly. "Yeah. I definitely want to hear about college, and, if I didn't say so, that wig is amazing."

I primp the long, wavy ombré locks. "Why, thank you, Sheriff Harper."

He resumes the attack on his burger, and I bring him up to speed on my archaeology lecture, how Silas performed as a professor, and the cool kids clamoring to be in my group project. And, for once, our timing is perfect.

He wipes his mouth as I finish my tale. "So, this group project . . . You have to do that tonight?"

"Oh, yes. I have to head back over to the dormitories and hang out with Brooklyn, Hutton, Kaden, and at least three others, to put together a critique of the late professor Klang's fascinating book, *Norse Expansion in the New World*."

Erick chokes a little on his sip of soda pop. "Are those people's names or places?" He wipes his mouth and shakes his head. "Man, I do not miss college."

"They're names. I'm starting to feel like being named after a ball of Greek cheese is too basic."

He grins. "Never."

Brushing away his compliment, I ask, "Did you go to BCCC?"

"Nah, back in the day, my mom scrimped and saved and insisted that I go to a big state school down south. It was fine, but I honestly learned way more useful skills while I was managing personnel and battle strategies in the Army."

"Hey, what's this 'back in the day' nonsense? You're not that much older than me, but that sounds a lot like my experience. The fantasy of film school was a solid five stars, but the reality was barely a two-star experience."

His easy laughter warms my heart. "So, you could say it was a 'would not recommend'?"

"Can confirm."

The momentary levity fades, and Erick walks back toward the bars to hold my hand while he shares the rest of his news. His voice carries too much worry. "About the ME's report—"

I tilt my head. "The medical examiner's report will help us. Whatever she found gives me more to work with."

"Oh, you'll have plenty to work with. The report was basically inconclusive. Cause of death was most likely blunt-force trauma to the occipital, that's the back of the skull."

"Hey, I know where the occipital bone is. I'm a crime-TV junkie, remember?"

"Of course. Anyway, the rest of the injuries, superficial bruises and cuts, were deemed the result of the broomball fights. Technically, the blunt force trauma didn't appear to be fatal, but with his history of concussions, it could be the cause."

"Could be the cause? So they don't even have a confirmed cause of death and you're still sitting in this cell! Oh, Silas is going to hear about this. We're getting you out of here."

He shakes his head. "Don't bother. The last thing I need is to be sitting at home explaining to my mom why I can't be involved in the investigation." He exhales dejectedly. "Plus, the report hypothesizes that the blunt force trauma is a result of the victim's skull impacting the ice at the rink."

"Wait! So they're still trying to pin this on you?"

Erick nods and squeezes my hand. "If that punch is what killed him, then I have to be held accountable."

"But they're not even sure if the ice rink is the murder weapon."

He laughs bleakly. "An ice rink as a murder weapon. I never thought I'd live to hear that phrase."

I shrug. "You and me both. I think it's a bunch of baloney! It wouldn't be the first time that the medical examiner has made a mistake. In case you don't remember, she miscalculated the time of death during the investigation of my grandfather's

LIES AND PUMPKIN PIES / 71

murder. That little gem almost landed me in jail!" I throw my free hand in the air in frustration. "Silas is representing you, right?"

Erick knits his brow in concern, but nods.

"Perfect. The defense is going to demand a second autopsy. And the Duncan-Moon Philanthropic Foundation is going to make a hefty donation to Sheriff Erick Harper's defense fund. We're going to bring in the best forensic pathologist money can buy."

"That fancy foundation is just you, right?" Erick pulls me toward the bars and plants a soft kiss on my cheek. "Glad you're on my side, Moon."

I flip my luscious wig over my shoulder and kick out a hip. "Yeah, you're real lucky. Don't you forget it, Sheriff."

His chuckle sounds hollow as it echoes off the cold brick, but I know an exit line when I hear one.

Next stop, the Piggly Wiggly to obtain proper snacks for an all-night study sesh.

The grocery store is relatively empty, and, since I'm in disguise, I get a full greeting from the checkout clerk rather than the locals-only head nod.

"Welcome to the Pin Cherry Piggly Wiggly. Can I help you find anything?"

"I'm good."

Grabbing a handbasket, I head to the snack aisle

and load up with a variety of salty options. I finish off the basket with a couple bags of bite-size chocolate candies and grab a twelve-pack of caffeinated beverages as I walk toward the checkout.

When I arrive on campus, it takes a few passes around the quad to locate the signs for Manone Hall. Finding parking is an even bigger challenge.

The freezing temperatures mean that all spaces close to the dorms are taken.

I end up parking almost two blocks away. My "win" is that I don't have to lug my two bags of groceries through any snow. The big storm is coming—according to all the locals—but it's not here yet.

Of course, the front door of the hall is locked. Seems obvious now.

There's a nifty key card scanner to the left of the glass door, but I don't have a card.

Before I die of frostbite, a too-friendly jock returns from some sport or other and gallantly holds the door for me as I babble on about losing my stupid key.

"If you get lost again, I'm in room 239." He winks salaciously and jogs away.

I think we both know I'm too much woman for that little guy.

Fortunately, the elevator doesn't require a key card. Stepping out on the third floor, I search for room 333 and knock tentatively.

The door flies open, and laughter and loud music spill forth.

"OMG!" Brooklyn glances over her shoulder, tugs at her messy blonde bun, and announces, "Darcy's here, and she brought hella snacks, yo!" She turns back and grabs one of my bags. "Come on in. Grab a chair or a bunk."

I slip past her and flop onto an over-sized purple beanbag. This apparently qualifies as a chair. I have to remind myself that not everyone has a ridiculously wealthy Ghost-ma and a swanky apartment filled with fine furnishings.

"Darcy, your boots are like the best thing in life right now!" Hutton widens her kohl-rimmed eyes and drools over my footwear while Brooklyn tosses bags of snacks to eager hands.

Ainsley reaches down from the top bunk and her half purple/half mermaid-green textured bob temporarily covers her face. She catches a pack of cheese puffs, and sighs dramatically. "These are everything. I'm doing a no-carb thing right now, so cheese is like my savior."

Far be it from me to point out that there is basically no cheese in a cheese puff. Let the skin-and-bones girl have a night off. Time to pour on the *Darcy*. "Stop. You guys are too much. These boots are totally over."

Brooklyn drops onto a zebra-print throw on the

bottom bunk and rips into a bag of white cheddar popcorn. "I can't believe you brought so much grub. Do your parents give you a massive allowance or are you a Visa-card kid?"

Neither. I'm a rich heiress that can see ghosts and receive secret psychic messages in my magicked mood ring. Don't worry, I don't say that. Instead, I fan myself with one hand and say, "Massive allowance."

Ainsley and Hutton exchange a wicked grin. "Lush!"

The group is smaller than I expected. "I thought there were some dudes in our group. What gives?"

Brooklyn rolls her eyes, throws herself back on the lower bunk, and exhales sharply. "Ainsley is having a spasm about pretty-boy Kaden, so he's out. Tayton never misses hockey praccy, and he says we owe him one for some free tickets, or whatevs, and then there's Bodie . . ." She starts giggling.

The wonder twins join in, until the snickers reach a maniacal pitch.

I pop open a soda, take a slow sip, and wait for the hilarity to die down. "What do I need to know about Bodie?"

Hutton is the first to catch her breath. She pushes her thick auburn curls back and winks. "He's got a med card, you know?"

First I'm hearing of this Birch County policy. "Like, for weed?"

Ainsley shoves another handful of puffs in her mouth and nods furiously. "Yeah, he's like totally useless."

The bad news: fewer suspects for me to question. The good news: these chicks can't keep their mouths shut.

It doesn't take a psychic to predict that these three will easily spend the rest of the evening gossiping, leaving me without a paper to turn in to Mr. Willoughby. Even though I'm only pretending to be a student, I find failure unacceptable. Time to push my agenda.

"So, like, what's the deal with Professor Klang? The reason I transferred to this school was because of him. Is this new guy any good?"

The trio exchanges a conspiratorial smirk, but the unofficial spokesperson, Brooklyn, takes the question.

"Um, Special-K, that's our secret name for him, was like the hottest professor ever. He came from an Ivy League school, or whatever. He was super smart and stuff, but mostly he was so plush."

They collectively swoon.

If you can't beat 'em, join 'em. "Right? That's my whole deal. I was hoping to transfer in and get a TA position, or find some other reason to stay after class." I flash my eyebrows suggestively and struggle to ignore the nausea in my gut as I join in their lascivious chuckles.

"Yeah, even though Bodie is AFK like eighty percent of the time, the other half of the time he was always sucking up to Special-K." Hutton scrapes her wavy locks back into a casual ponytail and pulls a scrunchy off her wrist to hold the hairdo together.

For all you non-gamers out there, AFK stands for "Away From Keyboard." Sadly, there's no time to correct her 80/50 math. Out of nowhere, my *moody* ring envelops my left hand in an icy chill. I glance down and, as the wisps of black mist clear within the glass dome, the image of a cow crystallizes. The image alone doesn't mean a whole lot, but my clairaudience picks up on the word *Ainsley*. Now I need a clever segue.

"What about you, Ainsley? Were you hot for teacher?"

She blushes and shakes her head in an entirely non-committal maneuver, but she avoids any eye contact.

Brooklyn pipes up with the truth. "No. Little miss farm girl is fully hot for Kaden. The only reason she even changed her major to archaeology was to be in more classes with her all-American hero. Obvs." She nods knowingly and rolls her eyes.

Ainsley throws a stuffed Pachimari down on Brooklyn and exclaims, "Shut up, B! It's not like that."

I hastily interject some reason. "Why does Brooklyn call you 'farm girl'?" Hopefully I'm on the right track.

Ainsley brushes the mermaid-green bangs out of her eyes. "My dad's like a big-deal dairy farmer. Brooklyn thinks it's hilarious to mention it at every possible opportunity. It's not like I live there now, you know? I live in the dorms like everyone else. I don't milk cows before I go to class anymore."

Brooklyn presses a fuzzy purple pillow to her abdomen and laughs uncontrollably. "Anymore!" She attempts to add to her clever quip, but her giggle fit prevents any further brilliance.

Yeesh! Can I get some useful information? "Were you guys close to Special-K?" Hopefully using their lingo will strengthen our budding bond.

Hutton's face grows somber, and she wipes an invisible tear from the corner of her heavily lined eye. "He was so gorgeous, you know? It's so cringe that he's, like, dead and stuff."

Oh brother! She and Grams would get along great. The horrible tragedy of handsome people dying! "What happens to his special projects? I was really hoping to get in on an active dig, you know?"

My extrasensory perception hums as Ainsley

leans away from the group, and the sensation of her fear of discovery thickens the air.

"Ainsley, is everything all right?"

She peeks over the edge at Brooklyn for permission to speak and gets the nod. "The six of us were like his archaeology Defenders. He was going to take us all on—" She breaks into tears and can't finish.

"How did he end up in Birch County? I heard he was a professor at Princeton or something?"

Brooklyn squeezes the pillow snug against her midsection. "He was the youngest professor ever to be named department head at Durham. Then the whole Kensington Runestone thing completely crashed his rep. At least they, like, gave him the option to resign, but he couldn't get hired anywhere after that. I guess he knew someone up here, or whatevs. So he got hired at BCCC—but he was still salty about the conspiracy, you know? He was, like, badmouthing those British people and claiming that one day he would prove the runestone was on the right track, even if it was a hoax."

"On the right track? What does that mean?" I lean toward Brooklyn, perhaps too eagerly.

Ainsley's energy shifts deeper into the vibration of fear and panic.

Brooklyn moves to the chair at the study desk

and gives her a nearly imperceptible headshake. And I say nearly imperceptible, because obviously I'm perceiving things on more levels than they can imagine. That was an unmistakable hush gesture from the Queen of the hive.

I push a little harder. "Seriously, what are you guys talking about?"

Hutton risks stepping into her own power. "He was, like, super obsessed with finding evidence of Vikings and stuff in North America."

I point to the book on the floor between us. "So this Norse expansion book . . . It's all theoretical?"

Ainsley whispers, "At the time."

Brooklyn snatches the book from the floor and grabs her laptop. "Look, it's late and we have to turn in this paper, like, tomorrow. The three of us already pretty much know this whole book by heart, so let's knock this thing out and crash. I need a solid six or I'll have wicked eye bags."

The sensation of finality floods through the room.

I'm definitely not going to get anything else tonight. I'm proud of myself, though. I made an impressive start and I have some juicy tidbits to work on.

To be fair, Erick is stronger than I give him credit for, and he'll figure out how to hang on while

I find the truth. I'm desperately hoping that the truth points a nice clear finger at someone else. There's no place for blurred lines in this investigation.

CHAPTER 7

GHOST-MA HAS DONE a bang-up job of setting up the murder wall. As I lounge on the settee and write out cards for each of Special-K's ring of Defenders, I wonder if there are any additional broomball rivalries I should investigate. It seems unlikely that a bunch of kids killed a professor they worship. However, I'm not ready to write them off just yet. Any potential suspects, besides Erick Harper, are worth further scrutiny in my book.

I grab the tacks and put the six new names on the corkboard. Using the green yarn, I connect them all to Gerhardt Klang. A handsome man, by all accounts, in his early thirties with a towering form in peak physical condition. Not sure about the heavy beard, but maybe it was a nod to his Viking obsession.

As I conjure up a variety of scenarios hypothesizing the size and strength of his attacker, my fiendish feline leaps onto the coffee table and silently deposits a piece of plastic.

"It's a little late to be logging things into evidence, Pyewacket." I reach toward the stretched remnant from a clear plastic bag and attempt to decipher the logo, or what remains of it, between the puncture marks of my wildcat's teeth.

There's a distorted image of a grinning cartoon polar bear and the words, "HILLY BEAR?" I stare at Pyewacket and shrug. "Sorry, big boy, I got nothing. I'll keep it in mind though."

Morning comes far too soon, and the prospect of finding Darcy another knockout outfit does not entice.

"Don't worry, dear. I've got everything handled."

Sitting up, I rub the sleep from the corners of my eyes and scowl at Grams through half-raised lids. "Lips not moving. Ghost get out of head."

"Understood, sweetie. When you're ready, I have a lovely outfit laid out for you in the closet."

Oh brother! I can't believe the apparition-entitlement I have to endure. Not even a half-hearted apology?

She clears her ethereal throat, and I glare a warning.

After splashing some cold water on my face and throwing a thick robe over my pajamas, I'm greeted by my impatient caracal.

He drops into a casual seated pose and looks away, too above it all to beg for human assistance.

I receive his silent message loud and clear. "Yes, Master."

Stumbling down the spiral staircase, I feed the beast and brew a cup of coffee to tide me over. Silas agreed to meet me for breakfast at Myrtle's before we take our separate vehicles to the college.

Back upstairs in my "super closet," Grams has laid out a pretty bangin' outfit. The black skinny jeans slip nicely into a pair of riding boots, which will be far easier to walk in than yesterday's footwear selection, and the silk thermal shirt will keep me extra warm, while being carefully hidden under my cashmere boyfriend sweater.

The thought of "boyfriend," even in relation to a sweater, conjures images of Erick. Our private forensic pathologist should have the second-opinion report today, and I sincerely hope it clears Erick.

Time to get some yummy in my tummy.

Silas gives a brief nod as I enter the diner, and Odell offers his standard greeting through the orders-up window. My news about the special group of six students that served as some sort of secret archaeology club doesn't carry the shock I'd imagined.

Silas smooths his grey mustache and nods. "That fills the gap between what I know and what I assumed."

This guy is always talking in riddles. "Maybe I need another cup of coffee, but can you explain?"

Silas harrumphs. "After the lecture, I took the liberty of searching Professor Klang's office. He had an unusual number of locked cabinets for a community college employee. Several contained unremarkable items, such as manuscripts in progress, rare texts, and a journal. However, an entry in the journal led me to seek out a hidden compartment in his desk. That compartment contained an artifact of Norse origin."

"Well, he did literally write the book on Norse expansion. Is it so strange that he would have an artifact?"

"In this instance, yes. Unless I am severely mistaken, this particular unicorn-horn-and-meteorite chalice was part of a traveling exhibit that originated from a small dig on the eastern shores of Newfoundland."

"Unicorn horn? Is that a joke?"

Silas waves away my disbelief. "It has since been shown to originate from the tusk of a narwhal, but the 'unicorn horn' was thought to possess powerful magic."

"So you think this relic is stolen? Are you saying Klang was some kind of art thief?"

"I do not believe that is exactly the scenario. In fact, it is far more likely that he was either part of the team that uncovered the original site, or he may have purchased the item with some of the grant money he received before the Kensington Rune-stone disgrace. Additional research is required."

I take a long sip of my perfectly brewed wake-up juice and savor the warm liquid as it trickles down my throat. "So what gap did I fill with my information about the Defenders?"

"Ah, yes. The journal. He made a series of cryptic entries regarding a secret project and an angel investor. He never mentioned the other members of his team by name, simply referring to them as 'the defenders of historical truth.' I believe you stumbled upon those persons involved in his quest for vindication."

Finishing my golden-delicious home fries, I wipe my mouth and slide my cup to the end of the table for Tally's "nick of time" refill. "Thanks, Tally."

"Did you do something different with your hair, sweetie?" She doesn't wait for a reply, but bobs her flame-red bun and hurries to the table by the window to refill another local's mug.

I brush the wig back and chuckle to myself. "It's

starting to sound like these students were more than hero-worshipers? Do you think they were actually involved in a working dig?"

Silas shakes his head and his jowls waggle back and forth. "I do not presume to know any concrete details of the group's activities. However, the entries in the journal indicate an elevation in Professor Klang's certainty, a much-needed infusion of cash that would help move things forward, but also the uprising of a seemingly immovable obstacle. It is precious little to go on, but if this immovable obstacle is in fact an individual, that individual may have had reason to halt the professor's inquest—permanently."

"Like, another suspect? Someone with an actual motive?"

Silas carefully wipes his mouth and mustache before answering. "Indeed. A suspect worthy of further scrutiny."

Glancing at my phone, I slide toward the end of the booth. "I better get going. What can I do to help us get to the truth faster?"

"I believe your current efforts to ingratiate yourself to the possible members of this secret club is our best option. In addition, our autopsy results will be available at the end of the day. Let us hope the new report provides another potential avenue."

"I do hope so. I'll meet you at the station after class. We can give the news to Erick together."

Silas nods, and I hurry off to school.

The lecture hall seems fuller today. Professor Willoughby is writing the presentation order on the whiteboard. As I make my way down the steps, Brooklyn turns and waves me to the front row.

Hutton, her auburn curls hanging loose, sits to her left and Ainsley is in the second row, snuggled onto the shoulder of the raven-haired man-boy who must be Kaden.

Asleep in the back row with his feet on the seat in front of him is surely the infamous stoner, Bodie.

Finally, I'll warrant a guess that the jock with the blond mullet on Kaden's right is Tayton. I pause for additional "extra" information to reveal itself, but nothing pops into my head.

Brooklyn removes her backpack from the seat next to her. "I added some stuff to our paper this morning. Needed a little kick, you know?"

As I drop into the available chair, I nod and smile. Like my mom always told me, if you don't have something nice to say . . .

"We will begin with the presentation on Professor Klang's book. I understand he was a renowned expert in Norse expansion." Remarkably, Silas sounds entirely sincere.

I stand, expecting the rest of the group to follow

suit. Instead, a volley of whispers, giggles, and head-shakes ensues.

In the end, Brooklyn and I are elected the de facto representatives of our ragtag band.

We step behind the podium, and Brooklyn lays the paper on the birch-wood surface. She begins to read the paper aloud—verbatim.

It's all coming back to me now. The memorization, the regurgitation, the lack of original thought. All the wonderful reasons why college was such a shattering revelation.

There has to be a way to unearth something useful in this sea of wannabe archaeologists.

I casually flip the paper over.

Brooklyn stutters to a halt. "What are you doing?" she hisses as she tucks a loose strand of blonde hair behind her ear.

Leaning toward her, I whisper, "Follow my lead."

A tentative smile curls the corners of her full lips.

"Actually, Kaden had some insight into what motivated Professor Klang to pursue his exploration of Norse expansion."

Ainsley's eyes are wide as saucers and she leans away from Kaden, while I gesture toward him. "Can you share your insights with the class?"

He crosses his arms over his chest and scowls. "Not cool, Brooklyn."

She shrugs her shoulders helplessly.

Beneath the tension, my extrasensory perceptions pick up a mishmash of emotions. The group holds a secret. It may be nothing more than what Silas has already uncovered in the journal, but, with a priceless artifact of questionable provenance in the mix, I intend to find out if anyone in this room knows about that possibly pilfered piece of history.

"My bad, Kaden. I thought you were, like, in the inner circle. I thought you knew about what he found."

Bodie wakes up in the back row. "Dude? Seriously? I thought I was your bro?"

Kaden shoves his way out of the row and marches up the stairs past Bodie's seat. "New girl doesn't know what she's talking about. We're out of here."

Tayton looks like a lost puppy. He definitely wants to follow his bros, but I'm assuming there are some academic requirements that hockey players must meet. A failing grade in this class would certainly impact his eligibility.

Turning toward Professor Willoughby, I attempt a save. "Sorry, Prof. I'm still learning everyone's names and I clearly got mixed up. That's totally on me. The group wrote a super awesome paper. So you should definitely base their grade on that paper, and if anyone needs to take a hit for this hot mess of a presentation, I'll totally take one for the team."

Tayton nods, and, unsurprisingly, no one in the group argues with me.

"Very well, Miz— Miss Brown. You shall receive a zero for this assignment, and the other members of your group will receive a grade based on my review of their critique. Return to your seat."

Ouch-town. Population: me. I didn't expect Silas to be so brutal, but hopefully my self-sacrifice will gain me some much-needed "street cred" with the Defenders.

The other groups don't fare much better than the Defenders and me.

Everyone is eager to beat a hasty retreat at the end of class.

"Miss Brown, may I speak to you for a moment?"

Tayton stops on the stair above me and turns. "Thanks for grabbin' the slot in the sin-bin for that wack presentation. My GPA can't take another yard sale."

"No problem. Catch up with you guys later. I got this." I have no idea whether any of Tayton's hockey slang is good or bad, but he started with "thanks," so I think I did him a solid. Embracing my role as martyr, I let my shoulders slump and my steps slow as I return to the front of the room, casting worried glances over my shoulder.

Ainsley takes one last desperate look before ducking out with the rest of the group.

"What's up, Silas?"

He harrumphs, possibly for effect, but more likely as part of his consistent disappointment with my lax etiquette. "Follow me."

His tone is a tad serious for a ruse. I hope he's not planning on actually punishing me for failing to make a pretend presentation, under an assumed identity, in a cover class, at a college I don't even attend!

The thin, wood-grain plastic plate on the door says Gerhardt Klang, but, since Silas produces a set of keys, it doesn't take a psychic to predict that this is now his office.

"Is his stuff still in there? Doesn't he have any family or anyone?"

"The department secretary has put in a request for boxes. I generously offered to pack up Mr. Klang's belongings when those boxes arrive. There has been no official request from survivors, and the college must clear the space in preparation for a permanent, full-time archaeology professor." He pushes open the door and gestures for me to enter the immaculate room.

"Oh, right. You're doing such a bang-up job, I forgot it wasn't your real gig." My quip brings an actual chuckle to Professor Willoughby's face. "You are performing quite well yourself, Miss Brown."

I feign a curtsy. "I'm guessing you didn't bring me here to discuss packing. My experience consists of filling a black trash bag with a bunch of worn-out clothes, or, post foster care, throwing a few things in a backpack before running out on past due rent."

Silas shakes his head. "The Foundation has taken care of all your outstanding debts. It was your father's suggestion, and a wise one at that."

"No argument here. It's not that I didn't want to pay my bills, but barista money and crappy tips only stretch so far. I'm much better at managing my financial situation now."

Silas exhales. "Indeed, since it is in fact I who manage your financial situation."

"Rude." But I have to chuckle at his accurate summary.

"However, I did not bring you here to discuss packing or finances. I'd like you to use your gifts to examine the room and its contents before they are carted off to a storage facility to decompose in anonymity."

"À la *Raiders of the Lost Ark*," I offer.

The languor of Mr. Willoughby's thin eyelids is a clear indication that he does not get my reference.

"I'll see what I can do." Rubbing my magicked mood ring encouragingly, I take a few deep breaths to clear my head of distractions. Starting to the right of the doorway, I make my way around the room, pausing to examine photographs, artwork, certificates, and other items as I move in a counterclockwise pattern.

Silas sits patiently in a visitor's chair, with his fingers steepled and his jowly chin bouncing rhythmically on his pointer fingers.

Nothing of interest is coming to me until I draw near the desk. *Deadly secret.* There it is again. "Silas, it's the second time the words *deadly secret* have come to me in relation to Klang. Where's the artifact?"

He opens the top left-hand desk drawer to retrieve the item he'd previously pulled from a secret compartment.

He leans over and searches with increasing intensity. "Unfortunately, it is gone. I placed the item in this drawer before we spoke and now it is missing."

"Well, I guess we know why he kept it in a secret compartment."

Silas narrows his gaze, and a flicker of his alchemical power stirs his aura like heat rising off Arizona pavement in the summer.

I take a step back and swallow. "Sorry, I didn't

mean that to come out as insultingly as it did. Where's the secret compartment?"

He removes the bottom drawer on the left-hand side and I kneel to examine the compartment behind that drawer. "That's clever. This drawer's a little bit shorter—"

"Incorrect. All the drawers are the same size. If one drawer were shorter than the others, it would be a clear indication of a secret compartment. However, with all drawers the same size, there would be no reason for the casual observer to suspect that anything is amiss."

"Copy that." I reach my hand in and let my psychic senses guide my feelers. They discover the concealed latch, and the compartment pops open. Again, I let my fingers do the walking. Along the top edge, I feel a strange shift in texture. As I slide my pointer back and forth over the spot, I recognize what I'm touching. Flopping down to my belly, I carefully use what little fingernail I have to grip the edge. Pulling out my find, I show it to Silas. "A negative."

Silas smiles like a proud parent.

Holding the single 35mm negative to the window, I examine the exposure. "It's a little girl—" As soon as I say "girl" a flood of images assault my senses. When the unbidden montage ends, I inhale sharply and lay the negative on the desk.

"What did you see?" He sits in absolute stillness.

I rub a hand across my forehead, and a shiver grips me before I reply. "The items are all Norse artifacts. The picture wasn't taken in a museum. The artifacts are piled on a coffee table. It's someone's . . . home!"

CHAPTER 8

IN EVERY MOVIE I've ever seen, when two or more phones PING simultaneously, it is not good news.

Silas for the win. "Ah, it would appear our forensics report is ready. Shall I drive?"

"As much as I love you, *Professor*, there's no way I'm riding in a 1908 Model T in this weather. I'll drive."

The Pin Cherry Harbor morgue is not a place I've been before, nor is it a place I'd ever like to visit again. For a budding psychic, such as myself, the pervasive energy of death and the confusing cacophony of "last" messages are overwhelming.

The ever-vigilant Silas must sense my unease. "Would you prefer to wait in the car? I can retrieve the report and we will discuss the results en route to the sheriff's station."

"That sounds—" Without bothering to finish my sentence, manners be dashed, I race back to the Jeep and get the heater running.

Silas returns in under five minutes.

I want to think positive, but the churning in my gut carries a visceral warning that's difficult to ignore.

Silas climbs into the vehicle with an upbeat smile lifting his round cheeks.

"It's good news? Your face makes it seem like it's good news."

"Whether the information is good or bad will be determined. However, it is complete."

This man and his hairsplitting! He could employ an entire race of follicle-based lumberjacks! "I accept your terms. What's the news?"

"The cause of death is no longer undetermined, nor is it in any way related to blunt-force trauma. In fact, the victim suffered two blunt-force trauma injuries in similar regions of the occipital on the same night. The examiner's best estimate is that the injuries were inflicted approximately two to three hours apart. The angle of impact varies, as does the velocity."

Faking a loud snore, I pretend to wake up. "Get to the good part. All of this nonsense about nonfatal blunt-force trauma is putting me into a trance."

"If Gerhardt Klang's death is what you refer to

as 'the good part,' then here it is. He died of a fatal embolism."

My extensive television-based education merely gave a cursory explanation of embolisms. "That's an air bubble, right?"

"It is. However, this particular air bubble was not a result of natural causes."

"What's that now?"

"Based on her expert analysis, the bubble of air that stopped Professor Klang's heart and starved his brain of oxygen was artificially induced."

And this is where Movie Medicine 101 fails me. "And by artificially induced, you mean . . .?"

"The local medical examiner did not see the need to perform certain tests. Our forensic pathologist performed a post-mortem CT scan, which revealed the air bubble, and, after removing the victim's thick beard, as part of a thorough search, she found an injection site into the external jugular, under the mandible."

"So, someone shoved a needle in his neck and pumped him full of air? And that killed him? Death by air?"

"I believe 'death by air' is the simplest explanation." Silas smooths his bushy mustache.

I'm smiling from ear to ear, but the sludgy feeling in my tummy refuses to vacate. No problem, I'm happy to continue to ignore it. "That obviously puts Erick in the clear. The death was clearly pre-meditated. Erick simply got in a fight with the guy after a broomball game. He didn't make an elaborate plan to devise a method of murder that would escape detection."

"Perhaps. Although, it did escape *initial* detection."

Nervous laughter battles with the doubts creeping along the edges of my mind as we drive to the station.

Silas and I nod politely to the deputy manning the front desk, and he stops at Erick's office to inform Deputy Paulsen we're visiting his client.

She nods. "Deputy Baird is processing the paperwork. Sheriff Harper is free to go." To be fair, her tone carries a note of relief. However, she can't leave well enough alone. "What's with the getup, Moon?"

Sucking in a quick breath, I open my mouth to sling a stinging retort her way, but Silas places a warning hand on my arm as he fields the question. "Miss Moon is undercover. We'll fill you in after we share the good news with my client."

I want to do a happy dance in the hallway and tell her to get her polyester-clad behind out of his office, but some of Silas's lessons have actually rubbed off. I withhold my celebration and, instead, imagine where I'll take Erick for dinner.

Silas regards my self-control with mild amusement.

Leading the way down the hall, I open the door into the holding cells.

"We have the new medical examiner's report! You're in the clear, and Paulsen is processing your release papers. Your self-inflicted quarantine is over. Dinner at the restaurant of your choice, *Sheriff* Harper."

Erick gets to his feet and ambles toward the bars. "Before I get my hopes up, let me see the report."

Silas passes the recent information through the bars and Erick paces a tight circle as he reads. The shift in his energy extends through the bars like the tentacles of a deep-sea creature. Each circle he makes tightens the invisible constriction of my heart.

"What's wrong? It's good news. It was clearly premeditated murder. Nothing to do with the fight or the ice. You're—"

Erick collapses onto the metal bench and crumples the report into a ball.

"Mr. Harper, what troubles you?" Silas grips a cold metal bar.

"There's a gear bag in the trunk of my cruiser. The vehicle is county property. They don't need a warrant. Please tell Deputy Paulsen that she'll find

a hand-pump with an air needle affixed to the noz-
zle." His head hangs. "Sometimes we have to pump
up the balls at practice, and the compressor at the
rink is always blowing a fuse." He tosses the
crushed report to the floor, lies back on the metal
bench, and laces his fingers together behind his
head.

He doesn't look at us. He doesn't say goodbye.
He stares at the cement ceiling and breathes in and
out through clenched teeth.

Silas grips my arm and gently tugs me away.

And that's what I get for ignoring the horrible
churning in my gut.

Outside the holding cells, I make my play.
"Silas, I'm sure I can pop the trunk on Erick's vehicle. You head into Paulsen's office to distract her
and I'll make that gear bag disappear."

Silas inhales slowly and his stooped shoulders
square as he rises to his full, powerful height. "You
will do no such thing, Mizithra Achelois Moon.
Erick Harper is an honest man who has chosen to
do the right thing. I will not stand by while you
sully his good intentions with your misguided
plots."

The words vibrate through my body, and the
folly of my deception is revealed like a centipede
under a lifted rock.

"Sorry. Honestly, I'm sorry. But I know Erick

didn't do this, and it's killing me to see him suffer needlessly."

My mentor smiles warmly and places a comforting hand on my shoulder. "You and I will uncover the truth. In the meantime, we must settle matters with Deputy Paulsen. Perhaps you can see your way clear to include her in our solution. I believe that while her hands are bound by the law, her loyalty lies with the sheriff."

I roll my eyes. "As if."

Silas narrows his gaze and a wave of energy shimmers around him.

"All right! All right. I'll try."

He leads the way into the office that Paulsen occupies and places his weather-beaten briefcase on a chair. He rummages around inside and retrieves a second copy of the report, which he hands to Deputy Paulsen. "My client wishes to cooperate with the investigation and has informed me to instruct you to retrieve a gear bag from the trunk of his cruiser. He indicated the bag contains a hand-operated air pump, with a needle attached."

Paulson stares at Silas in confusion before running her pudgy finger down the pathology report in an attempt to decipher his message. "So he's confessing to the murder?"

That's it. End of rope reached. "No, he's not confessing to the murder, Paulsen. He's not guilty of the murder! You and I both know that. He's co-operating with the investigation. Clearly someone is setting him up!"

Paulsen drops the report on the desk that does not belong to her and crosses her arms stubbornly. "Look, Moon, I follow the evidence. If the evidence leads to Harper, I'll arrest him. I'm not saying that's where I want it to lead, I'm telling you how I run a legal investigation."

"What are you implying, Paulsen?"

She tilts her head with an irritatingly superior slant. "Another thing that you and I both know is the way you slip around the edges of the system." She gestures to my wig and scoffs. "You seem to think that the laws don't apply to you." She rises to her full five foot two inches. "Well, I'm here to tell you the law applies to everyone, even Sheriff Harper. If the murder weapon is in his gear bag, I will place him under arrest for suspicion of murder."

As I lunge forward, the unexpectedly strong arm of Silas Willoughby bars my path. "None of us will move any closer to discovering the true villain if we waste time squabbling amongst ourselves." He looks over his right shoulder at me, and his eyes spark with a fiery warning. Satisfied that his message is received, he returns his gaze to Paulsen. "If you will permit it, Deputy Paulsen, I would encourage you to allow Miss Moon to bring you up to speed on what she has uncovered at the community college."

I gasp and find myself at a loss for words. How can Silas throw me under the bus like this?

To my shock and awe, Deputy Paulsen's arms fall limp at her sides and she drops onto the chair with a sigh. "Something smelled rotten from the minute this got called in." She shakes her head. "According to dispatch, the call came from an untraceable number, despite the fact that the Zamboni driver claims he's the one who found the body."

Slipping past Silas, I slide onto the empty chair beside his briefcase. "Why wouldn't he have called from his own cell phone? Does he have his number blocked?"

Paulsen leans forward. "Absolutely not. I placed a test call to dispatch from his phone and the number showed up—no problem. There was also no previous call to dispatch in his call history."

"That's shady." I chew my bottom lip for a second. "So he placed a call from someone else's phone and has no memory of it?"

"He kept saying he found the body. He never actually answered me when I asked him if he placed the call."

"Weird."

Paulsen leans back in the chair and nods her head. "Definitely."

Land o' Goshen! I think Paulsen and I are working together. It's not terrible. I'm sure I could make a lot more progress if I had her cooperation than if I had to sneak around and obtain everything less than legally. "What do you say, Paulsen? Call a truce, just this once?"

She nods unconvincingly, but offers me her hand.

I grasp it, and seal the bargain with a handshake.

"I shall leave you two to discuss the potential suspects in the archaeology class. I must request some additional information from the pathologist. My findings will be shared the moment they become available."

A weak smile graces Paulsen's face. "Thanks, Willoughby. You always were a straight shooter."

Silas bows his head in gratitude, retrieves his beat-up valise, and exits the station.

After bringing Paulsen up to speed on my findings, we agree (I'm as shocked as you) that my continued presence at the community college could reveal additional leads.

In the interest of getting things off on the right foot, I chose to leave out a few details, like the secret compartment in Klang's desk and the missing uni-corn-horn cup.

Once I get the negative of the little girl developed, I'll turn it over to Paulsen as an additional gesture of goodwill. I don't have to tell her exactly when I uncovered it. That's part of my mysterious charm.

Time to head over to the *Pin Cherry Harbor Post* and see if Quince Knudsen is home from college for Thanksgiving break.

Right after I take off this blasted wig and give my poor scalp a good scratching!

CHAPTER 9

THE LOCAL JOURNALISTIC house of integrity is showing its age. Winter-dormant vines steadily consume the brick corners, and the painted letters are fading from the plate-glass window. The logo appears to read: "Pin herry Harbo Pos ."

As I run across the street, an arctic wind whistles up from the great lake and bites my cheeks and nose. Luckily, I found a spare stocking hat in the car, to hide my disastrous post-wig hair and cover my tender ears. The metal handle on the glass door is so cold I can feel my bones icing through as I swing open the portal and rush indoors.

Previous visits to the newspaper have taught me not to expect a welcoming committee. I slide into the office behind the counter to see if Quince is in the adjoining darkroom, where the pungent odor of acids and ammonia lurks.

No such luck.

I'm forced to return to the lobby and ring the bell resting on the birch-clad counter. Much to my dismay, the elder Knudsen emerges from the depths.

Blink. Blink. Blink.

The juxtaposition of the diminutive man's height compared to the size of his eyewear never ceases to amaze. The massive lenses magnify his eyes to comical proportions.

"Good afternoon, Mr. Knudsen. I'm not sure if you remember me? Mitzy Moon."

His small mouth cracks into a grin beneath his enormous glasses. "I believe your philanthropic foundation was responsible for establishing a photo-journalism scholarship at the local high school. My son, Quincy Knudsen, was the fortunate inaugural recipient. I'm not sure if you're aware of Quincy's photographic accomplishments, but—"

"Quince and I are well acquainted. I'm so glad to hear he received the scholarship." I also happen to know that this man will literally never stop talking if left uninterrupted. "The reason I'm here today is because I need a negative printed. I was hoping to pay Quince for a quick turnaround. Do

you happen to have someone helping you with photographs while he's away at school?"

Blink. Blink. Blink.

The issue with this man seems to be that he has
trouble engaging his starter, but once the engine is
running, he has that "1970s muscle car" tendency
to run even after the ignition is in the off position.

"Negative you say? Are you referring to a
35mm negative or perhaps you have a vintage
camera with a 110 cartridge—"

"It's a 35mm negative, Mr. Knudsen. Do you
have someone?"

"There was a girl that was helping on Mondays
and Wednesdays, but her younger sister's best
friend had an incident at her after-school care
provider—"

"Oh, how unfortunate. Is she here?" This man
will be the death of me.

"The girl? Oh, no. It's Friday."

I nod and smile. "Do you know how to make a
print and develop it?"

Blink.

"I'm sure someone must've taught Quince."

"Why, yes. When did you say you needed this
print?"

"How about we get into the darkroom and develop it right now?"

"Well, I have to proof the stories for tomorrow's edition. And I still have to write the *Letter from the Editor*, so I am—"

"I tell you what, why don't you go and print this negative for me, and I'll draft up a letter from the editor for you. What were you planning on writing about this week?"

"Let's see . . . I believe folks should be prepared for the big storm. It's always good to stock up on canned goods, dry goods—"

"Agreed. I'll put together a wonderful storm-prep letter, and you can add your special touches. Deal?"

Blink. Blink. Blink.

I hand him the negative and smile as I gently steer him back toward the darkroom.

He shuffles and I follow. While he steps into the black cylinder that rotates and dumps out its occupant in the light-proof darkroom, I take a seat in the dilapidated office chair and open up a new document on the museum-piece computer.

He hums a jaunty tune as he works, and for some reason the sound of it seeping out of the photo lab infects me with a severe case of the giggles. The image of the tiny man in his large glasses, singing as he skips around the darkroom, reminds me of a children's story that should never be written.

Since I know next to nothing about prepping for a winter storm, I force my psychic senses to replay several enhanced memories from the diner. Regulars are always chatting about the weather, and no weather seems to get as much attention as storms. Once I've played enough clips to gather the required intel, I type up a rough draft and sign it "The Editor." I don't actually know Mr. Knudsen's first name, and that's not for lack of interest. It's straight-up, stone-cold fear. I'm afraid that if I ask his name, he would begin by saying, "In the beginning, Adam begat Cain and Abel, etc." I'm not sure I have time for that genealogy.

The cylinder scrapes around with a swoosh, and Mr. Knudsen emerges, holding a black-and-white 8 x 10 print and my negative, now in a protective sleeve.

"Thank you, Mr. Knudsen. Your letter from the editor is on this computer. I wasn't sure if you wanted me to print it out."

"You're already done?"

"Well, it's a draft. I wasn't sure how long it needed to be, but I think it's a good start."

He shuffles over to the computer and pushes the chair to the side. At his height, five feet in boots, he doesn't need to sit down to get a good look at the screen.

"What do you think?"

He puts up a hand, indicating he's still reading.

As I wait for his feedback, my mood ring tingles on my left hand. I glance down at the photo and grin. It's unmistakably Ainsley, circa 2005 CE, sitting cross-legged on a coffee table next to a pile of what appears to be authentic Norse artifacts. "I better be going, Mr. Knudsen. Thanks again for this print, and please say 'hi' to Quince for me when he gets home next week."

He straightens up and turns. "You're very fast."

"Thanks, I think." I resist the urge to snicker or mumble, *That's what he said.* "Let me know if there's anything else I can do. I sure appreciate this photo. Bye now."

I can practically hear his eyelids blinking as I hurry out.

There are so few days left before everyone heads home for the break, I better get back over to the dormitories and see if I can pry Ainsley away from the herd. Of course, that means I have to get back into the wig. Aargh!

Lady Luck smiles upon me when I arrive at the dormitories. A gaggle of giggling girls are clustered around the front door. One of them taps their key card against the scanner, and, when they all start filing in, I join the conga line.

They continue on toward the common area and

I break left to the elevator. Up on the third floor, I meander down the hallway reading the various stickers, Post-its, and miniature whiteboards on the wooden doors. Eventually, I find one with the following message: "Ainsley. Had a late study sesh. Don't wait up. Hutton."

Knocking firmly on the door, I hope it sounds friendly and not like the resident assistant's knock.

"Hutton isn't here."

"Ainsley? It's— Um, it's Darcy. I was actually looking for you." Holy *Bourne Identity*! Forgot who I was for a minute there.

Ainsley opens the door, and her expression is one of confusion as she scoops her green bangs out of her eyes. "Me? Why would you be looking for me?"

"Can I come in?"

She steps back hesitantly. "My room's not as nice as Brooklyn's."

"No sweat. Brooklyn's room is a little over the top, if you ask me."

Ainsley instantly jumps onto this train. "Right? Like, that zebra comforter is cringe."

"Totally." I scan her room for anything I can possibly compliment. "You have a lot of books. I knew you were the smart one."

Her eyes sparkle and she blushes. "Thank you so much. I thought college would be me, living my best life. I didn't expect to spend every day in someone else's drama, you know?"

"Totally." Oh brother. I've got to come up with another response. "So, I'm pretty sure Professor Willoughby is going to throw down a pop quiz on Monday. He seems like the type, you know? Sounds like a lot of people are taking off this weekend and adding a few extra days to their break, and I think he wants to make sure they take a hit in their GPA."

"For reals? That would be bad. Like, super bad. You better go. I need to study."

Wow, she may not be as brilliant as I assumed. "Yeah, that's why I'm here. I thought we could study together. I mean, I'm so new and I've missed so much—"

"No way! You crushed that identification exercise. You are, like, pro-level. But, yeah, let's study."

Smile and nod, Mitzy. "I saw the note on the door. Does Hutton stay out late studying very often?"

Ainsley turns and rolls her eyes dramatically. "Hutton? Studying on a Friday night? That's such a load of cow manure. And, trust me, I know cow manure." She chuckles at the self-deprecating reference to her farm upbringing.

After a forced courtesy laugh, I ask, "Oh. Where is she?"

"Her and Brooklyn are— They don't think I know. I mean, it's not a big deal."

My psychic senses finally kick in. "You don't think they're with Kaden, do you?"

"Yeah. Kaden is totally stepping out on me. But the joke's on him, or at least it was."

Right as I'm about to snatch a juicy extrasensory tidbit about her slimy boyfriend from her subconscious, her walls go up. "What do you mean 'was'?"

"Skip it. Stale doughnuts. Let's just study, okay?"

Foiled again. Time is running out and I can't afford to be patient. Time to push the boundaries. "Do you have any soda? I mean, pop? Or water?"

"OMG! I'm so sorry. You brought all those super lush snacks the other night and I'm, like, not giving you anything. I'm such a potted plant."

"Don't worry about it. I wasn't trying to be all that, but I'm kinda thirsty."

She grabs two glasses, which may or may not be clean, from the counter above the mini-fridge, and pulls a two-liter bottle of root beer from the middle shelf. "Is root beer okay?"

"Totally." That word is like sour milk in my mouth. I hate the sound of my own voice.

She fills the two cups and passes one to me. I take my glass and follow her toward a low table between the two bunk beds, where all of her books are haphazardly stacked.

As I walk behind her, I sink my finger into my root beer and carefully trace the truth symbols that Silas so painstakingly taught me. As I focus on drawing the symbols accurately and in the correct order, I can hear his voice echo in the back of my mind.

"This is no parlor trick. This is a powerful transmutation, and you should know better than most how truth can be a double-edged sword. It is not a skill to be abused. It is a potent tool, to be wielded with the precision of a scalpel."

She sets down her glass and turns to organize the books and make room for me.

I place the alchemically transmuted cup of root beer next to hers and swap their positions like a sleight-of-hand magician. Part of me feels a flash of guilt, but the rest of me is absolutely all right with doing whatever is necessary to get to the truth. I keep the untainted glass in hand and take several big sips, hoping that my thirst-quenching act will encourage her to take a drink.

Finally!

She downs half the glass in one go.

That's my girl. "So what do you think Hutton and Brooklyn are really doing tonight?"

Her eyes widen, and her mouth seems to move

despite her efforts to prevent it. "Brooklyn's secretly dating Kaden. She thinks I'm too stupid to notice."

"That's rude. Why did you say it doesn't matter?"

She blinks and a brief flash of fear darts through her eyes. "Everyone thinks I transferred to archaeology because of Kaden, but it was really because of Special-K. Kaden is—was—just his errand boy, or whatever."

I'm starting to regret my decision to use any means to get at the truth. "What do you mean?"

"Like, I was kind of— It all started online. I kind of had a thing with the professor."

She may be eighteen and everything, but I definitely have to hide my shock and focus on keeping her talking. "I get it. He was super yummy. How did you meet a professor online?"

"No, I met Kaden in this online dinosaur game. He invited me to his Jangle server for a private chat and said he was into archeology for real."

"That's cool."

"I guess. Whatevs. I tried to impress him by saying that I had authentic Viking stuff and then he wanted to MIRL."

"Merle? Who's that?"

"OMG, Darcy. Isn't it obvs? Meet In Real Life. Kaden wanted me to bring one of the artifacts and meet him on campus."

Her energy is struggling against the truth symbols and time is running out. "Did you meet him?"

"When I got there, Special-K was there. I was kinda swoony. I showed him this ultra-fancy cup. He said it was the goddess Freya, carved into a unicorn-horn chalice, and he touched my hand and— He was super smart, and he was totally gonna prove his theory about Norse expansion. I was helping him on a secret project. He had this investor that was going to fund our dig, and the cup was gonna be, like, collateral. He said the two of us were going to *remake* history."

"I thought all the Defenders were helping him?"

Her eyelids slide open so far I fear her eyeballs may pop out of her head. "You know about the Defenders' secret project?"

"That's why I came here. Professor Klang invited me to be part of the group." I sincerely hope she doesn't ask me too many questions, since I have zero information about the inner workings of the Defenders.

She narrows her gaze and a thick wave of suspicion rolls toward me. "Show me."

"I'm afraid I can't do that. You'll have to show me yours first." Again, totally spitballing here.

She reaches into the pocket of her skinny jeans and produces a runestone that looks like it's carved from a piece of antler. The symbol is a "Y" with an extra line in the middle. I recognize it from one of Silas's books, but I don't remember its meaning. "Now you," she says.

Great. The stress is shutting down my psychic talents, and I clearly have no runestone to show her. Time for some B-list acting.

I *accidentally* spill my soda on her textbooks.

She panics and drops the stone as she struggles to rescue her books.

"I'll grab some paper towels. I'm so sorry. I'm such a stupid klutz." I scoop up the stone with my left hand as I run toward the kitchen.

She's desperately clearing away her papers and flicking sugary liquid from the textbook covers, but calls after me, "Don't even. It's my fault. I usually don't bring soda in here."

Shoving the runestone in my pocket, I grab a wad of paper towels from the roll. But, as I walk back, a strange whispering swirls up my spine toward the nape of my neck.

Trust only me. Trust only me.

I toss the wad of paper towels at Ainsley as the overwhelming need to climb out of my own skin consumes me. "I'm super sorry. I'll buy you new textbooks or whatever. I've gotta go! I forgot I have to pick up my cat from the vet before they close."

Racing down the hall toward the elevator, I

claw the runestone from my jeans and drop it in the pocket of my puffy jacket. The whispering doesn't cease entirely, but it's quieter. I can resist it.

I scramble into my Jeep, fishtail out of the parking lot, and gun it back to the bookstore.

CHAPTER 10

My HEART IS POUNDING in my chest like a war drum, and I can't seem to catch my breath as I pull the heavy metal door closed behind me and lock myself into the bookstore. Now that I'm safely home, I grab my phone and shout for Grams while I dial Silas.

She pops into existence right in front of me as Silas answers the call.

"It's a bit late to be calling your professor for extra credit." He chuckles over the speaker and Grams smiles along with him.

Unfortunately the next two words out of my mouth will seriously murder their mood. "Rory Bombay."

Silas grumbles. "On my way." The line goes dead.

Grams swirls around me protectively. "What do you mean, Rory Bombay? Is he here? In this bookshop? He's dangerous, Mitzy. We're not prepared. I'm not sure if the protections Silas put in place all those months ago will still hold up. What should we do?"

"I'd say we should take a deep breath, but only one of us needs oxygen. Take it down a couple notches on the paranormal panic dial."

Ghost-ma crosses her bejeweled limbs over her designer gown and tilts her proud head. "You don't get to march into my bookshop, drop that man's name like a used handkerchief, and then tell me to calm down."

I raise my finger in protest. "Correction, *my* bookshop. I appreciate everything you left me in the will. However, by definition a 'last will and testament' means the end of one thing and the beginning of the next thing. I'm the *next* thing."

"Oh my, I would've expected a little more gratitude, especially this time of year."

I wag my head back and forth. "Fair point. And since we'll be waiting until Silas gets here to dive into this Rory Bombay mess, maybe this is a good time to talk about Thanksgiving?"

"What do you mean by that?"

"Well, Dad asked me if I had any plans. Which,

of course, I don't. I haven't had holiday plans since my mother was killed. I'd love to spend Thanksgiving with Dad and Amaryllis, but I'd like Erick to be there. If he's out of jail by then."

"He better be! I'll haunt the hind end off that Deputy Paulsen—"

"Easy, *Atomic Blonde*. I think we were talking about Thanksgiving."

"Oh, well in that case, Twiggy always does Thanksgiving."

"Always? I don't remember anything about it last year."

"You were new in town. I think she took the dogs and went to visit her sister. It was an odd year for everyone. Kind of a reset year, if you will. But now you're here to stay and a tradition is a tradition. You better check with Twiggy before you make any plans. Also, ask her if she can host the meal here. I don't think it's fair to leave me out."

"All right." I bow with a flourish. "The last thing I want to do is put a burr under Twiggy's saddle or exclude a ghost that can't eat!"

Grams giggles and her shimmering hand pushes playfully at my shoulder.

It's an odd sensation to be touched by a ghost, but there's so much love in her energy field that it almost always brings a smile to my face.

"Mitzy, we may have been gifted with too much junk in the trunk and a random assortment of psychic gifts, but neither of us got any patience. Tell me what happened! You can give Silas the shorthand when he gets here."

"Copy that." I slip out of the puffy jacket, hold it away from myself as though it's a poisonous snake, and carry it upstairs to the apartment.

By the time Silas arrives, I've filled Ghost-ma in on all the interpersonal relationships between Professor Klang's inner circle of acolytes, plus the added bonus of a possible teacher-student affair, and we've placed a 3 x 5 card bearing Rory's name on the murder wall. To be clear, it's not his first appearance on my infamous corkboard of suspects.

"Good evening, Mizithra. I do appreciate the key. Thank you for seeing to that."

Grams zooms down to our level and Silas shivers with a quick flash of ghost-chills.

He reaches into one of the many pockets inside his tattered tweed jacket and slips out his special spectacles. Carefully unfolding the wire arms he hooks the brass curves behind his preternaturally large ears and scans the room for the phantom. "You are looking well, Isadora."

She smiles and gestures for me to bring him up to speed.

"So the connection between Ainsley and Professor Klang definitely deserves further investigation, but the *pièce de résistance* is this." I reach for the puffy coat, tip it sideways, and shake until the runestone clatters onto the coffee table.

Silas reaches toward it.

"Don't touch it. You taught me well, Mr. Willoughby. That little beauty is as cursed as cursed can be, and the mantra that it chants is very reminiscent of a charm previously used by the devious Mr. Bombay."

Silas withdraws his hand and nods at me approvingly. "It gives me great pleasure to note that my lessons are not in vain."

I brush away his compliment with a flick of my wrist. "There will be time for praise later. What I need to know is can you break this curse or uncurse this stone?"

Silas smooths his mustache with a thumb and forefinger. "To what end?"

"Oh!" I slap the heel of my left hand on my forehead. "Did I not mention that every one of the Defenders has one of these cursed runestones? Or at least that's what I assume. Possibly only Ainsley's stone is cursed, but with all the weird stuff going on, it makes more sense that if this token is a symbol of membership to the inner circle, all the tokens are cursed."

Silas points to the mark etched on the surface of

the cursed stone. "The rune of defense. Used as a tool to control. A clever and deadly ploy. Certainly of the type we've come to expect from Mr. Bombay."

"This is what I'm saying. I'm ninety-nine point nine percent sure he's the mysterious 'angel investor' you found mentioned in the journal. But I need you to uncurse this one so I can use it as my buy-in to the inner circle and find out for certain. Can you do it?"

He lowers himself onto the scalloped-back chair, steeples his fingers and bounces his chin on his pointers.

I exhale and pace around the murder wall/corkboard.

While each of us is engaged in our own mental gymnastics, neither of us notices the furry fiend slinking along the perimeter.

Out of nowhere, Pyewacket leaps onto the coffee table, drops something from his mouth, and hisses vehemently at the cursed runestone. He leaps off the table and runs to hide underneath the four-poster bed.

"What did you bring us, Mr. Cuddlekins?"

Grams swirls closer. "That's my smart boy." She floats off to congratulate him, while I take a seat opposite Silas and wait for his input.

The chin bouncing stops, and a brief smile

flickers beneath his bushy mustache. "Ah ha! A solution comes from a most unlikely source."

Looking back and forth between the two runestones, the cursed one, and the one delivered by Pyewacket, doesn't bring a matching smile to my face. "I get that they have the same symbol, but they look nothing alike. That smooth, wooden one isn't going to fool the Defenders. Can you fill me in on the good news, Silas?"

He pats his round belly and leans back with a satisfied sigh. "The obliteration of a curse is a next to impossible task. The energy used to create a hex cannot be destroyed. It can be transmuted, but some portion of the curse's original stain may always linger. A much simpler and efficient method, as Robin Pyewacket Goodfellow has shown us, is transference."

"Sounds great." I smile halfheartedly. "What's transference?"

"It is the process of moving energy from one place to another. If I can move the curse from this runestone to the one Pyewacket provided, I have a means to keep the curse intact, while freeing the original item from any negative influence. The more similar the two items are in size, shape, and intent, the easier and more permanent the transference."

"You done good, son," I call to the whiskered

face peeking out from under the dust ruffle. "He's not gonna pull that cursed-item malarkey on us."

"Re-ooow." Not in my house!

Turning to my mentor, I offer my assistance. "What do you need from me?"

Silas gets to his feet and shuffles toward the Rare Books Loft. "I must consult a text or two, but I believe I possess all the ingredients required."

I bet he does! What I wouldn't give to get a peek at all the secret pockets in that man's jacket. "Will it throw off your mojo if I make some microwave popcorn?"

My use of the term mojo produces a hearty laugh from my mentor. "That should be fine. And if it's not too much trouble, I would love a cup of that hot chocolate that you brew."

"No problem." I'm sure he knows it's a packet mix, but I'm glad he likes it. I'm feeling very positive about our chances, and I skip down the treads of the wrought-iron staircase two at a time. In fact, my bravery extends to hopping over the chain at the bottom.

And, as the saying goes, "Oh Icarus, you flew too high." I manage to tuck and roll, and avoid any serious injury, other than my pride.

"Everything okay down there, Mizithra?"

"Yes. Please pretend you didn't hear that."

A ghostly snicker drifts through the ether.

"I'm warning you, Isadora. I can wear your vintage Chanel and forget to dry clean it at a moment's notice. Don't push me, woman."

She laughs outright, and my heart swells with love. It feels good to belong somewhere. To have people who answer my call for help and genuinely have my best interests at heart. I won't say it was all worth it to get to this point, but I will say the painful memories get a little dimmer each day.

The delicious smell of popped-buttery goodness fills the bookshop. Once upon a time, there was a terrible instance of burnt microwave popcorn, which triggered a silent alarm to the fire department and something called a halon fire-suppression system.

Thanks to my ghostly resident's hasty instructions, I was able to shut down the halon, but I was not spared an embarrassing visit from the, less than pleased, Fire Chief. So, I pop my popcorn for two minutes and twenty seconds—and not a second more.

I can handle a couple of old maids at the bottom of my bowl. Way easier than a ladder-truck full of apparently disappointed firefighters.

Getting comfortable on the settee, I toss a popped kernel in Pyewacket's direction.

He leaps at least eight feet in the air and

snatches the popcorn with the deadly precision of a laser targeting system.

Grams claps her hands, but adds, "I would hate to be a bird in that beast's line of sight."

Since my mouth is stuffed full, I simply widen my eyes and nod.

Silas clears everything from the coffee table except the two runestones. "I will require silence and concentration during this transmutation. No more feline aerobatics, and no otherworldly horseplay between you and your interfering grandmother."

I swallow my popcorn and make a face at Grams.

She giggles insufferably. "I best go work on my memoirs. I never behave more poorly than when someone tells me to behave well."

Chuckling, I share her admission with Silas, and he nods furiously. "Exactly my point. Good day, Isadora. All my best on finding a publisher for your life's story."

She vanishes through the wall and her disembodied voice calls out, "Tell him thank you for me."

"She says, thanks."

He harrumphs. "As with any alchemical procedure, it behooves you to pay careful attention. You may not be prepared or trained to perform such complex transmutations, but exposure to the processes will open new pathways in your psychic array."

Inexplicably, that speech makes me think of the Star Trek Enterprise. At least I possess enough awareness to realize this is not the time to share that tidbit with my mentor. "Copy that." I cross my legs, pull a cozy throw over my shoulders, and diligently munch my popcorn.

Silas produces three glass vials and a small metal tin from inside his coat. The two amber vials he sets to the left of the cursed runestone. The metal tin he sets to the right of the un-cursed runestone.

He lifts the clear-glass vial and removes the stopper. He pours three drops of clear liquid on the un-cursed stone. He replaces the stopper and slips the bottle inside his coat.

Next he opens the small metal tin. That type of container reminds me of the salve my mother used to rub on my arm when I would get too close to the jumping cholla cactus. Somehow the goo pulled the needles from the flesh and helped the wounds heal. Tangent! I lean forward to get a closer look at the contents. Fine jet-black powder. Yet, as I stare into the tin, the flecks seem to shimmer with a metallic nature.

He opens one of the amber vials and pours

white crystals in a circle around the two stones and the open tin.

My clairaudience hears *salt*. My eyes agree.

Silas places his hand over the cursed runestone and utters a rhythmic series of three Latin-sounding words. His hand pulses above the stone with each repetition of the chant. He pulls the stone's energy upward—forming an invisible ball.

All at once the invisible becomes visible, and it looks as though he holds a plasma globe beneath his right hand. Forks of purple, blue, and silver lightning spark within the clawed grip of his fingers. He then moves that sphere of energy over the un-cursed stone and chants a new Latin phrase. This one he repeats twice and forces his hand down firmly.

The sphere of lightning detaches from him and spins around the stone like a spider encasing its prey in the threads of its silk. The energy tightly envelops the stone, and before my very eyes the two become one.

Silas draws a shaky breath, and for the first time I glance up at the man performing this ritual before me. The color has drained from his face and his stooped shoulders seem to bear a great weight.

I want to ask him if he's all right, but he gave me strict instructions not to speak.

He retrieves the final amber vial, pulls the

stopper, and gently pours one glistening black drop onto the formerly cursed rune. The liquid falls in slow motion, and when it touches the Defense rune it seems to be absorbed into the original etching, and travels down each ligature at equal speed. When it has completely filled the symbol, an audible pop emanates from the small disc.

A moment after the sound, Silas picks up the newly cursed runestone and drops it in the black powder. The fine ebony grains swirl in a counterclockwise tornado around the runestone.

I can't help but hold my breath, and I'm certainly not able to eat any more popcorn.

The tiny cyclone swirls on and the silver flecks bounce in the light.

Silas picks up the lid, and floats it above this miniature storm. I watch in awe as the storm sucks the lid down with ear-popping pressure. He breathes a sigh of relief and drops, exhausted, into the scalloped-back chair.

"So, that was amazing, but you look spent. What do you need?"

"I'll take that hot chocolate now."

"Oh, right." I jump up and race out of the apartment, down the stairs, and zap the cup in the microwave for a thirty-second hotter upper.

My distraction with hot-buttered goodness got

the best of me earlier, and I left the cocoa on the table in the back room.

When I return, some of the color is coming back into his cheeks. I hand him the mug, handle first, because I still got mad tolerance for hot mugs. Barista skills, you never really lose them. I toss a few more kernels toward Pyewacket, but he's lost the thrill of the hunt and waits until they hit the carpet to casually retrieve them.

"Can you explain what happened? And what everything is?"

He takes a long sip of the hot chocolate, wipes his mustache, and exhales. "Certainly. The clear vial is holy water. To remove any residual energies from the target object. We don't want the curse to be altered in any way."

"Got it." Not gonna ask him where he sources his holy water. He'll tell me if I need to know.

"The second vial is salt. This particular formula is specially created to set a firm boundary which the energies cannot cross."

I nod, pretending I understand that there are different kinds of salt.

"The third contains alchemically altered squid ink, which protects the cleansed runestone against re-contamination."

Despite my best efforts, I can't help but murmur, "Squid ink. Cool."

"The canister contains a finely crushed dust comprised of activated carbon and ferric oxide. It anchors the cursed object and allows the energies to be contained within the metal clamshell."

"And the swirling cyclone?"

He smiles and his eyes twinkle. "A bit of showmanship."

My eyelids pop up like a breakfast pastry out of a toaster. "Silas Willoughby, you showboater."

He bows his head. "Perhaps you should check on your grandmother. I do need a moment to rest."

When I reach the third floor of the printing museum, Grams is hunched over her writing desk and utterly oblivious to my presence.

I'm certain she's using that fancy quill pen to forge my signature on another batch of query letters, but I'll let it slide. I hope she finds a publisher for her precious memoirs. She'll be the first ghost to top the New York Times bestseller list—or will she?

What an odd thought. I can't possibly be the only person in the world who can communicate with ghosts, which means she can't possibly be the solitary ghost. Is that comforting or creepy? Is there a club? A secret society? Oh, the possibilities are making my head spin.

It's best if I leave her to her craft and return to Silas.

Blowing her a silent kiss and wishing her luck, I

thread my way through the large printing presses on the first floor and return to the apartment.

"Ah, Mizithra, would you escort me to my vehicle?"

"Sure. Everything all right?"

"Indeed. I wish to return home and partake of my restorative tinctures. You will keep me posted on any news of our foul friend?"

"Count on it."

CHAPTER 11

THE BOOKSHOP IS CLOSED for the weekend, and possibly even on Monday. Twiggy headed south to scoop up a treasure trove of rare books at an estate sale that she's had her eye on for some time. When I pointed out that it's morbid to circle like a vulture above a dying animal, waiting for a well-known book collector to pass through the veil, she assured me it was a common practice in our line of work.

Since I have zero knowledge about collecting rare books, and it's more her line of work than mine, I'm in the unenviable position of needing her more than she needs me. So I nodded my agreement and offered to pay for her trip.

She scoffed away my generosity and hung a "Closed for Collection Trip" sign on the front door.

Generally, the empty bookshop feels safe and

adventurous. The scent of possibility fills the air, and shelves and shelves of books speak of other worlds and other lives. However, amazing escapes at my fingertips don't have the same frivolous intrigue with the possibility of Rory Bombay slithering around in the shadows—nothing is truly safe. I have to keep busy to prevent my mind from spinning out of control.

Today, I'll head down to Grand Falls to see if Bombay Antiquities and Artifacts has had any recent visits from its absentee proprietor.

A scratch at the alleyway door flicks all of my senses into high alert. I tiptoe toward the door and press a hand to the cold metal. "Pyewacket, is that you?"

"Reow." Can confirm.

I unlock the heavy deadbolt and push the door open a crack. "What are you doing outside? It's freezing. Actually, let me rephrase that question. How did you get outside?"

Pyewacket struts past me and straight into the back room. He rests on his haunches, looks up at me, and tilts his head with an air of superior tolerance.

"Never mind. You go out when you want to go out. Who am I to question the activities of my feline overlord? Let me get you some Fruity Puffs."

He waits patiently while I grab a bowl and dispense a portion of his guilty pleasure.

I have no idea what he does or eats when he's outdoors, and I am perfectly fine keeping it that way.

Opening the cardboard flaps of a leftover container, I inspect the sweet-and-sour chicken. "Smells okay to me." I pop the container in the microwave and brew some coffee while my breakfast reheats.

Ghost-ma drifts in, looking especially vaporous.

"Everything all right, Grams?"

"I had a breakthrough."

This may be my first spectral existential crisis. "Care to share?"

"I was making some edits on my memoirs. As I read through several chapters, covering three different relationships, I was struck by the idea I may have been a tad self-involved."

Thank heavens I don't have a slug of coffee in my maw, because there would be a very large spray of java covering the back room on that spit take. "This is a revelation?"

Her apparition shimmers. "I was a busy woman, Mitzy. I was on the boards of several charitable organizations, and I traveled extensively collecting arcane texts for this bookshop. I didn't have a great deal of time for self-reflection."

"And now?"

"Well, I have all the time in the world now, don't I?"

The idea generates a slow ache in my heart. "But I don't."

"What do you mean? Did someone threaten you?"

Shrugging, I reach for my cup of coffee and retrieve my breakfast from the microwave. "It's nothing. I need to eat."

Grams peers into the partially open container. "I must say, I don't miss eating as much as I thought I would."

I pull out a chair and pick at the best pieces of chicken from my day-old Asian experiment.

Grams chuckles. "Day-old? Whatever you need to tell yourself, dear."

"I believe we were talking about you, Isadora."

"Oh, yes. You enjoy your coffee while I— We can discuss my spiritual growth later. I'm concerned about your doom-and-gloom outlook. We'll always be together, sweetie."

"I don't think so. When I die, I'll cross over like most people. If you're tethered to this bookshop, I'll never see you again."

Grams flickers in and out of focus. "When the time comes, I'm sure Silas can reverse my situation."

"Silas? You think Silas will still be alive when I

die? Do you know something I don't about his longevity, or are you expecting my demise a lot sooner than I am?"

Grams taps a perfectly manicured finger on her coral lip. "I hadn't— I assumed— I need to make some notes." And without so much as a "good luck hunting for bad guys," she pops out of sight and I'm left with my subpar breakfast, my lukewarm coffee, and some afterlife anxiety.

"What about you, Pye? Do you think I'll have any luck tracking down Rory Bombay?"

He pauses in his ablutions, with one large tan paw in mid-whisker swipe. He looks like a tiny feline villain in an old silent movie.

"No comment?"

As an afterthought, his golden eyes fix me with a warning, and he gives a halfhearted hiss.

"Copy that."

Upstairs, I layer up for the day's adventures and pull my pilfered handgun from the back of the scarf drawer.

I'm not sure whether I hope to find Rory or hope not to find him, but either way I want to be prepared.

With sweaters and a thick winter coat padding my person, shoving the gun in the back of my waistband doesn't seem like a plan for easy access.

The large pockets of my puffy jacket will have

to do. Checking to make sure the safety is on, I slip the Springfield EMP in my coat.

Phone, keys, and I'm out the door.

Heading south, toward Grand Falls, the dark clouds thin by the time I reach the antiquities shop, and a pale blue sky shines with the light of a crisp winter sun.

As I case Bombay Antiquities, I'm surprised to see that it's open.

It never occurred to me that the estate sales and antique collecting would continue in Rory's absence. I park a block and a half away and cautiously approach the shop.

Before going in, I scroll through the contacts on my phone and select the direct number to the sheriff's station, slipping the cell into my pocket—at the ready. If he's here, I'm not going to try to be a hero. I'm calling for backup on the spot.

I push open the door, take a sudden interest in vases, and struggle to ignore the smell of mothballs.

"Welcome to Bombay Antiquities. Is there anything in particular that I can help you find?"

That hint of a Southern drawl sounds vaguely familiar. Seems like Rory kept more than Gershon's inventory of antiquities when he scooped up the business after the previous owner's sudden death. "Oh, I need to browse a little."

The petite redhead steps from behind her immaculate Louis XVI desk and daintily crosses the room as quickly as her snug, narrow pencil skirt will allow. "Don't I know you? Seems like you've been here before." She puts a hand to her forehead. "Ah, yes. You purchased a collection of armed services medals, if I'm not mistaken."

Wow. This chick is no slouch. Although, to be fair, there aren't a lot of twenty-two-year-olds, with pure white hair, frequenting antique shops. Time to see if she's as innocent as she sounds, or if she's Rory's accomplice. "Oh, yes. That was a while ago. How's business been?"

No change in her energy.

"It's a little slow this time of year, but there have been some lovely estate sales. We're fortunate to have several new items." Her voice is almost as soothing as a kitten's purr.

Maybe a more specific query will trigger her defenses. "Does the owner collect items from out of state or are all of these antiques local?"

Still no shift in her general vibe.

"We bring in objects from all over the world." Her gentle smile widens. "I rarely see the new owner. He travels extensively. I handle the local business and he ships items from abroad whenever he finds something he thinks will suit his clientele."

"How nice. He really trusts you to keep an eye on things here."

A whisper of defense floats upward. "I do my best."

"Have you received any shipments recently?"

The invisible defense thickens, and she shifts her stance. "Let me see." Her smile remains sweet and her eyes bright, but she chews her bottom lip thoughtfully.

I sense that she's stalling. "Nothing new?"

"Let me check." She steps behind her desk, and one hand shuffles a stack of papers from the left to the right.

"You take your time and think about it." Maybe she's pressing a button that sounds a silent alarm. Better make good use of my remaining time. "I hate to ask, but is there a restroom I could use?"

She's definitely uncomfortable now. "Well, it's technically not for customers." Her soft Dixieland charm is wavering.

"Gosh, I'm in need of several things for my new apartment. I'm sure it would be worth your while if I could stay and shop without being so distracted." Dangle the ol' money carrot. That should work.

"It's through that door there. Mind your step. I'm unpacking some things in the back."

"Thank you so much." The singsong emphasis on "so" is a little snark I learned at college. I step through the door and reach out with all of my senses. Is he here? Did she send him some kind of message?

A quick scan confirms she has definitely been unpacking a new shipment. I snoop through the items, but there's nothing of interest and nothing cursed.

Much of the storeroom is carefully organized, and several of the items are shelved with certificates of authenticity or carefully notated provenance tags.

Circling around the second set of shelves, I walk back toward the restroom. There's a lamp on at the work desk in the corner.

Pulling out my gun, I click the safety off and approach slowly. So much for my promise to "not be a hero."

The lamp is very hot; the bulb has been on for some time. I slip around the desk where a copy of *Norse Expansion in the New World* is open to the chapter on Newfoundland.

The top left-hand drawer is ajar. My claircognizance fills me with a strong sense of knowing that something of importance lies within that drawer. I slide it open carefully, and in an instant the message is confirmed.

The chalice of narwhal tusk, etched with an image of the goddess Freya.

How did it get here?

A light scraping comes from somewhere beyond the shelves, and my skin crawls with fright. If I take the item, he'll know I was here. But if I leave it . . . It might be a critical component to some scheme he's building.

What would Silas do?

Take it.

The phrase resounds inside my head, and I shove the object inside my puffy jacket without a moment's hesitation.

The door from the retail space opens. "You all right, Miss?"

I carefully push the drawer closed, flick the safety on my gun, and shove it in my pocket.

Tiptoeing away from the desk, I make my way down the aisle before I reply. "I think I got turned around. I don't see a bathroom over here."

Her heels click rapidly on the cement floor and her eyes are bright with concern when she rounds the corner. "You shouldn't be back here." Her gaze flicks nervously toward the desk, and her sweet down-home Southern accent has vanished. She's angry, and a little afraid.

"I'm so sorry. I'm terrible with directions. I have ambulatory dyslexia. If I'm moving at all, I don't seem to know my left from my right. Could you point me in the right direction?"

She squeezes her eyes closed for a moment as

she struggles with my wearisome presence, and recovers her charm. "It's right over there, sweetie."

"Thank you." I hurry into the bathroom, close the door, and lean against it as I catch my breath. She's been in contact with Rory. There's no mistaking that flicker of fear. Whether she stole the artifact from Klang's office or he did, someone has been doing some research.

I flush the toilet and turn on the taps to complete the ruse.

When I open the door, she's waiting with her arms crossed. "I didn't want you to get lost again. Let me show you the way back to the store."

Rude. "Thank you. I'm wondering if you have any Art Deco pieces?"

One grossly over-priced lamp and a hideous white panther bookend later, I've paid penance for my guilt. With no intention of further tempting fate, I hustle back to my Jeep with the packages—and my prize.

CHAPTER 12

SINCE GRAMS and I don't know a great deal about narwhal tusks, or their potential use in magic and alchemy, I opt to call in the big guns. Unfortunately, Silas is otherwise engaged. He promises to pick up doughnuts and coffee from Bless Choux in the morning and delve into a deeper Rory Bombay discussion at that time.

Pyewacket is deeply disturbed by the recovered relic, and circles warily around the coffee table. In the end, he takes up a position atop the wardrobe and sleeps with one eye open.

I've had all the excitement I can stand for one day, and a long hot bath with one of my new rainbow bath bombs is just what the doctor ordered. Or would be, if doctors gave orders for spectacular soaks.

"I'll search for that book while you're luxuriating in the tub, dear. The unicorn horn reference has a real ring of familiarity. One of the secretive arms of the Rare Books mezzanine must contain what I'm looking for. If I can't find it tonight, you can text Twiggy in the morning."

"Copy that, Grams. And to make sure we're all on the same page, there's no popping in the bathroom while I'm luxuriating in the tub. Capisce?"

Grams throws a sparkling hand to her forehead and pops a salute. "Aye, aye, Captain."

Oh brother. I grab my warmest pajamas, thickest socks, and my robe.

Pyewacket continues to feign sleep from his perch, high atop the antique furniture.

Splendid steam fills the bathroom and the wall heater hums to life. This has to be the coziest space in all of Pin Cherry Harbor.

The bath bomb emits a warm spiced-apple fragrance as it circles around the bathtub sputtering its rainbow trail. Eventually we get to the end of the rainbow, and I slip into the delicious liquid.

Resting my head against the soft, air-filled pillow suctioned to the back edge, I replay the incidents at the antiquities shop to see if I can collect any extrasensory information about the suspicious events in the back room.

Starting the memory-clip with my hand on the

front door, there's a strange flash of familiarity. I can't discern whether it's the place or a person, but it's worth noting. There are two or three items on the carefully lit shelves that draw my attention as I walk through the psychic recall—they scream *stolen*.

No surprise there.

I fast-forward to the moment when the pretty Southern belle steps behind her desk to check her inventory. The left hand shuffles papers, while the right hand slips out of sight.

The extrasensory replay allows me to zoom in and confirm that she indeed presses a button.

The light blinks on and off in the back room. I hadn't noticed that in the shop, but this tidbit supports my suspicion that she was alerting someone to my presence.

Fast forward to me searching the shelves and desk in the storage area. There's that sound.

I rewind the scene. With all of my inexplicable perceptions engaged, the replay reveals that the sound is definitely the shuffling slide of a foot. The energy is twisted in some way—almost as if it's masked. For me, that's authentication enough. Who else would be hiding in the back room of Bombay Antiquities and cowering behind a magical shield?

Allowing myself to slip under the water, I release the replay as the heat and fragrance envelop me.

Silas will know what to do.

Tomorrow.

Tonight's program includes: relaxation, recharging, and reheating—

"If you say reheating sweet-and-sour chicken, I'll find a way to ghost vomit!"

I shoot out of the water like a surfacing submarine. "Grams!"

The ghostly form has its back turned, for what that's worth. "I'm sorry, dear. I know I broke the rules, but I found the book, and I can't manage enough physical substance to pull it from the shelf. So when you're done in here—"

"Oh, I'm done. Trust me, relaxation obliterated." I lift the drain plug and scowl. "Skedaddle, so I can at least get dressed in peace."

"Thank you, dear. You are a treasure."

"Flattery will get you nowhere, you peeping ghost!"

She snorts as she vanishes through the wall.

Out on the elegantly curved left arm of the mezzanine, that long ago surrounded the huge brewing vats that were part of this historical distillery, I slide the ladder across the shelving to the point where Grams is bouncing up and down like a toddler who has OD'd on birthday cake.

"It's here. It's right here. See, *Unicorn Magic of the Norse*."

I climb carefully up the ladder, not wanting a repeat of the fall that could've killed me several months ago . . . but that's another story. Reaching the shelf where Grams is anxiously pointing, I toy with her for a minute. "Is it this book? This one right here?"

Her pointing finger becomes a fist and lands on her curvy hip. "Don't you get smart with me, young lady."

Laughing at my own joke, I retrieve the book and slowly back down the ladder.

The tales prove less enthralling than the title led me to believe, and I'm shocked awake when the voice of Silas Willoughby crackles over the apartment's intercom. I drifted off so quickly last night that the reality of daylight leaves me confused and disoriented. Surprisingly, I'm still holding the book of "unicorn" lore—or, rather, bore.

"Coming!"

"He can't hear you until you push the button, dear." Grams gestures toward the wall.

Not being a morning person, I glower and snap. "Thanks, Vasco da Gama. I've had the intercom orientation." I put on a false voice and recite the lesson. "The mother-of-pearl-inlaid buttons are the way to respond. The one on the left lets you talk and the one on the right is the 'call' button to ring the back room. The middle rings the museum."

Grams crosses her arms and tsks. "You had better adjust your attitude before Silas gets up here. He won't tolerate sass."

I push the button on the left and attempt some congeniality. "Come on up, Silas. I'm desperate for doughnuts."

Ghost-ma snickers behind me. "You should put *that* on a T-shirt."

Pushing the plaster medallion above the intercom, I turn as the bookcase door slides open for Silas. "I deserved that. Sorry for snapping at you. You know me— and *early*."

Grams crosses her bejeweled limbs and lifts her chin. Vindicated at last.

Silas enters with a large box of pastries and two steaming cups of java. He places everything on the coffee table and takes his favorite chair, as I lunge for a cup of black gold as though it's the antidote to a poison.

He speaks while I glug. "I uncovered a plethora of alarming facts. How did your research progress?"

Grams laughs openly at his query, and both of us glance toward the open book peeking out from under the folds of the down comforter.

"Not that great." I take another glorious sip of coffee before I continue. "I kind of nodded off. But, in my defense, it was the most boring book in the history of ever."

He carefully chews his pastry and politely wipes Bavarian cream from the corner of his mouth. "Which text put you to sleep?"

"Something about Norse unicorn horns . . ."

Silas nods. "Ah, yes. A fanciful attempt to disguise the truth. Once the myth of the unicorn horn had been put into play, narwhal tusks escalated rapidly in value. There would've been little benefit to hunters to correct the inaccuracy."

My bottom lip juts out in a mock pout. "So you're not about to tell me that unicorns are real? Because with all the ghosts and stuff, I was really hoping for unicorns."

Silas chuckles and reaches for a second pastry. "I wish for it as well. However, in the long years of my life, I have never had the pleasure to prove or disprove that myth. There are yet places in the world I have not visited. Perhaps, one day . . ." His musings are terminated by a mouthful of éclair.

Grams rockets down from the ceiling in frustration. "I think the two of you have had enough to eat. Let's get down to business. Why is Rory Bombay after that unicorn horn chalice?" She gestures violently toward the relic next to the doughnuts.

"Yikes. For your information, Grams is getting a

little pushy. I think we better wrap up breakfast and get down to the deets."

Silas smooths his mustache. "I'm not familiar with Dietz. Is this a relatively new author?"

The burst of laughter that erupts from my mouth carries a small puff of powdered sugar along for the ride. "Um, no. It's short for details. All this time at college has affected my vocabulary."

Silas harrumphs. "Not for the better, I see."

"You're not wrong."

"My time with arcane texts proved quite valuable. The chalice was carved from a narwhal tusk, the stem and ornate base were crafted from iron ore extracted from a meteor. The symbol on the cup is indeed the mark of the goddess Freya."

"So why does Rory want it?"

"Certainly not to transmute poison. It was proven in the 1600s that narwhal tusk, then known as unicorn horn, did not possess any properties of merit in that arena."

"So what's he after?"

"It is far more likely the power of this cup is linked to the seiðr magic instilled by the high priestess of Freya. According to my research, it is believed that this vessel once held the power of illusion. Perhaps it plays into a scheme of Mr. Bombay's to conceal himself from authorities."

I reach for a third doughnut, but Ghost-ma's

gasp forces my hand back to my lap. "So he drinks something from this cup and becomes invisible?"

Silas tilts his head back and forth slowly. "In a manner of speaking. It would be a complicated transmutation, resulting in an intricate delusion. I do not believe Mr. Bombay possesses the skill. However, he is delving deeper into these murky secrets than I would deem safe."

"Do you mean he could get sick, like what happened to Grams?"

She sputters with offense. "Look here, young lady, I wasn't devouring mystical texts in search of supreme power."

I arch an eyebrow and translate for Silas.

He leans back and chuckles. "I had no intention of impugning your reputation, Isadora. There was no malice in your search for knowledge. Perhaps you were a bit greedy and depleted your body faster than it could replenish. It's not a judgment. It is simply the truth."

Sadness and regret vibrate my grandmother's apparition. She floats through the wall without a word.

"She didn't argue, but she did leave."

"Understandable."

Picking up the chalice, I turn it in my hand and trace the gentle swirl of the unicorn horn. "Do these whales still exist?"

"Narwhals are severely endangered. Apart from the Inuit peoples, no one is permitted to hunt them in this day and age. This cup may, in fact, have powerful magical properties, but it is also worth a veritable fortune."

"Wow." I gingerly set the chalice on the coffee table.

"We must protect it and see that it is gifted to a museum for proper display."

"Sure. Whatever you recommend. I'm not really comfortable owning something made from an endangered species."

"Indeed."

"Should I go back to the antiquities shop and confront Rory?"

Silas leans into the over-stuffed chair and laces his fingers over his paunch. "That would be ill advised. One man is already dead. I believe we've uncovered a probable motive. I will continue my research here, in the loft. Tomorrow we shall see what we can pry from the lips of the Defenders. Perhaps today you can visit Mr. Harper and update him as you see fit."

"Am I giving any of this information to Paulsen?"

"Perhaps it is time to hand off the negative. A gesture of goodwill should keep her on our side."

"Copy that."

Silas retires to the loft to page through history, while I shove a judgment-free third doughnut in my mouth and finish my coffee.

Down at the station Paulsen is in an uncharacteristically foul mood, even for her.

"Hey, Deputy. I found something that may or may not help the case."

She scowls up from the mountain of paperwork on Erick's desk. "Look, Moon, I don't have time for hunches. The evidence against Harper is stacking up." She leans back and sighs heavily. "And despite what you think, I don't like that."

I nod and pull a small envelope from my coat pocket. "This negative was recovered from Professor Klang's office. I'm not sure if it will help, but it appears to depict some Norse artifacts. Maybe he was engaged in some black-market trading? It's a potential lead."

Paulsen takes the negative. "Okay. I'll get this over to the lab and get a print made." She puts one of her pudgy hands on the telephone and pauses. "Thanks."

"No problem. We both want the same thing, right?"

She nods and picks up the receiver.

That's my cue. I exit the office and walk toward the holding cells. The heaviness in my heart is sure to affect the expression on my face. As my hand rests on the door handle, I attempt to access some positive energy reserves and paste a smile on my frustrated face.

"Harper? You awake? I brought doughnuts."

His sexy fingers reach through the bars and grip the cold grey metal. "This promises to be the highlight of my day, Moon."

I smile and pass the doughnuts through the bars. My eyes widen as I take in the redecorated cell. "First it's prisoner makeover day, and now it looks like an episode of *While You Were Out*. What's going on in here, Harper?"

His cheeks redden, and he rolls his eyes. "You would be looking at the efforts of holding cell interior designer, Gracie Harper." He sits on the metal bench, now covered by a small mattress and a handmade quilt.

"Your mom is a pistol. If you're in here much longer, she's liable to paint a mural on that back wall."

The smile on his face is everything. "You have no idea."

Given Erick's history with Rory Bombay, I keep the update to the 35mm negative and a possible connection to black-market artifacts.

He nods, but I can feel his desire to jump into this investigation.

"I'll stop by after school tomorrow and let you know if Silas and I get any more info from the students."

He sets down his pastry and walks to the bars. His hand reaches through and brushes the snowy hair from my face. "It's nice to see the real Mitzy, too."

His kind words stir my heart, and my cheeks flush a self-conscious shade of pink. "Thanks, Sheriff."

He presses against the barrier and pecks my cheek. "Keep sayin' that. It gives me hope."

That one little phrase keeps me toasty warm all the way back to the Bell, Book & Candle, despite the howling winds and threatening clouds.

The remainder of my Sunday fun-day is frittered away listening to Silas drone on about narwhals and unicorn horns.

No smoking gun is revealed and we opt for calling it a day and hoping for a breakthrough tomorrow.

CHAPTER 13

THE COMFORTING WEIGHT of Pyewacket sprawled across my chest wakes me. As I scratch between his black-tufted ears, I offer my thanks. "I appreciate your protection, Pye. I'm sure you heard us talking about Rory—"

HISS.

"I couldn't agree more, but I'm a little scared, you know? He's already so many steps ahead of us. I don't think I can handle it if he gets away with murder—again. If there's anything you know that could help me, I'm open to all suggestions. Don't hold back, boy. I need all the players on my team to give me a hundred and ten percent."

A sparkling ball of energy slowly drifts toward the bed.

"Thanks, Grams. After the fright of discovering

Rory's back in town, I definitely can't take any of your apparition hijinks."

Ghost-ma twinkles into the visible realm and smiles warmly. "Pyewacket was on alert all night. He never left your side."

For some reason, this news chokes me up more than I would've thought. "Of course, that means you also never left my side."

She shrugs her designer-gown-clad shoulders and looks away.

"We're gonna get him this time. I don't care what inter-dimensional laws I have to break, Rory Bombay is gonna wish he never met me."

Grams floats up to the ceiling and her essence flickers pensively.

"What is it? I can tell something is troubling you."

She hovers near the tin-plated ceiling and gazes down at me. "Well, who's thought-dropping now?"

"Touché. But seriously, do you have any ideas?"

"Not yet. Give me some time and I'll definitely come up with something. For now, you should get to school and ask Ainsley about that photograph."

"The photograph! I completely forgot. When I felt the curse emanating from that runestone, I lost my mind and ran. She probably thinks I'm completely insane." I gently push Pyewacket to the side and throw back my thick down comforter. "You better have an extra special outfit for today. I'm gonna need to win friends and influence people faster than Carnegie ever imagined."

"I'm on it!" The ghost of grandmothers past blasts through the closet wall with the conviction only a fashion diva can hold.

"Come on, Mr. Cuddlekins. Let's go scrounge up some grub before I have to face the potentially cursed Defenders."

I slip into my fuzzy dragon-claw slippers and the two of us shuffle down to the back room. As I approach, I smell coffee brewing. "Twiggy?"

My heart shouldn't be looking for a place to hide inside my rib cage, but knowing that Rory Bombay is loose in Pin Cherry makes even the most mundane things seem suspicious.

"Yeah. What's up, doll?"

Whew. "Welcome back. Did everything go all right at the estate sale?"

Twiggy chuckles. "Well, look who's all interested in the business. Yep. I was the first collector on site and I had the good stuff locked up before JB's plane even landed."

"JB is another collector?"

She pretends to spit on the floor. "He's a washed up bookmobile chaser."

I don't think I want the backstory on JB. Time for a change up. "Grams said I should ask you about

Thanksgiving. I don't want to put any pressure on anyone, but my dad and Amaryllis brought it up, so . . . I don't have any plans."

She pours some questionably dated half-and-half into a cup of java and hands it to me.

Now I'm doubly suspicious. "Are you all right? You don't seem like yourself."

"Trust me, kid, I was already pouring the coffee. Don't go thinking you're special."

Now, that's the Twiggy I know.

"I always have a big potluck out at my place. Your dad and Amaryllis are more than welcome. Tell them to bring the pumpkin pie and you can bring rolls." She tilts her head. "And please, buy a bag from Piggly Wiggly. I don't want anyone breakin' a tooth."

"Gee, thanks. What about Erick and his mom? I mean, I'm sure I'll get him out of jail by then. There's no way he murdered anyone, and now that Rory Bombay—"

"Whoa! That good-for-nothing, green-eyed serpent is back in town?"

Swallowing, I nod slowly. "I'm ninety-eight percent sure. I found a cursed runestone in the dorms Friday night, and it's exactly his kind of tactic."

"You let me know if there's anything I can do. These biker boots are happy to stomp on anything that gets out of line."

We share a chuckle, and I nod. "Thanks. I'm kind of hoping Silas has a trick or two up his sleeve."

She laughs out loud. "That man has more tricks than either of us could count."

"Copy that."

"I'll feed the beast. You get changed for school, kid."

I shake my head and exit without reply.

The echo of her cackle follows me as I retreat to the safety of my apartment.

"All right, Grams, I had a few sips of coffee and I'm ready for whatever six-inch-heel-based outfit you've got planned. I'm at your mercy."

Her shimmering image appears at the closet doorway, complete with a smirk. "Perfect. Then I can't wait to show you what I've chosen."

Stepping through her, I glance at the pieces carefully placed on the padded mahogany bench.

"What do you think, dear?"

Tears spill from my eyes. "Every time I think I've got you figured out, you pull another supernatural trick out of your invisible back pocket. Thanks for believing in me."

"I'll never stop. I love you."

"I love you too, Grams."

She rushes off, and I run my fingers over the items she's lovingly chosen. My favorite pair of skinny jeans. My comfortable, well-worn high-tops, and a long-sleeved T-shirt with a picture of a cat filing one of its claws. Beneath the brazen feline it says, "Sure, underestimate me. That'll be fun."

I'm not ready to go full Mitzy Moon, so I bobby pin the wig into place. I feel practically invincible as I slip into today's wardrobe.

Silas is taking roll when I walk in. "Thank you for joining us, Miss Brown."

Five heads spin toward the door at the back of the room. The painfully obvious absence of Ainsley's face among the crew pricks a warning hum in my psychic senses.

Brooklyn's messy bun tips to the side as she gazes disapprovingly at my attire. "Those shoes are so cringe, Darcy. Did you oversleep?"

I don't have time for this girl's multitude of hang-ups. "Where's Ainsley?"

"Ouch. Down, girl." She glances at Hutton and smirks.

I look past her and address Hutton directly. "Where's Ainsley?"

Hutton twirls an auburn ringlet around her finger. "She was AFK when I got home last night. I think she bugged out early to add some vacay days to her break, you know?"

"No doubt," chimes Bodie.

I stride up to the lectern and whisper to Professor Willoughby. "Ainsley is missing and I'm sure it's no coincidence. Can you get the rest of the crew into your office and give me an opportunity to brandish my club membership?"

"Certainly, Miss Brown."

Returning to the seat next to Brooklyn, I plunk down and cross my arms.

Silas clears his throat. "Today is the perfect opportunity for field research. Return to your critique groups and visit one of Pin Cherry's historical sites. If you are unfamiliar with the area, the Pin Cherry Harbor Historical Society provides maps, free of charge. You will present these field reports on Wednesday, for half of your total semester grade."

Gasps of shock ripple through the student body.

Silas collects his things and walks toward the exit next to the whiteboard. "Oh, and Miss Brown, bring your group to my office at once."

Brooklyn rolls her eyes and adjusts her hair. "Great job. Now we're, like, totally going to get slammed with extra work."

She links her arm through Hutton's elbow and drags her out the door after Professor Willoughby.

The three male members of the group eye me

suspiciously and follow Brooklyn as though it was their idea.

Once we're all crowded into the late Professor Klang's office, I pull out the now un-cursed rune-stone I swiped from Ainsley and show it to the group. "I thought this was supposed to mean something. When Professor Klang invited me into this program, he assured me that the Defenders looked out for one another. I can't believe that Ainsley has been missing for almost twelve hours and none of you bothered to report it."

Shocked expressions adorn every face in the lineup, but no one else produces their stone.

"Maybe you guys aren't in the club? I assumed that since Ainsley was in the club, and she hung around with you . . ." I let my voice trail off and wait, hoping they take the bait.

Brooklyn produces her stone. "As if. Ainsley was, like, the last one to get a stone. And I'm not even gonna tell you what she had to do to get it."

Silas sends me a very clear, but invisible, message. My clairaudience hears the phrase *all the stones*.

Kaden fishes around in his front pocket and thrusts his runestone in my face. "See? BTW, you don't know what you're talking about, New Girl. Klang didn't give us these stones. The angel investor passed them out at a special after-hours meeting. He said that only members who had these stones would share in the profits from the dig's treasures. If we lost 'em, or whatevs, we got nothing."

"Well, let's see everyone else's. What I'm about to say is exclusively for the inner circle."

Hutton digs in her backpack, while the two remaining boys reach into their various pockets. Within seconds, five hands are extended forward to display five cursed runestones.

Silas mumbles something in a strange tongue, which I've never heard before.

The five Defenders go glassy-eyed.

"What did you do? Did you stop time?" I stare open-mouthed at the frozen coeds.

"It is a weak counter-measure that locks them in a temporary loop. Use these tongs to collect all the stones and place them in this pouch. Then you must quickly trace the reversal runes on each of their hands and erase their memory of this meeting."

"Seriously? You told me those symbols are incredibly dangerous and shouldn't be used willy-nilly, or whatever."

"Indeed. Time is running out to find Ainsley and catch Rory Bombay. In this instance, my powers must remain as secret as yours. You have little time. Start with the blond boy on the left and work quickly, but with deepest focus."

A chill creeps across my shoulders and the hairs on the back of my neck stand on end. Since solving my mom's murder, I understand that sensation means she's watching over me, and it bolsters my courage. I grab Tayton's hand, take a deep breath, and visualize the words and actions that took place in this room as I carefully trace the four symbols, in the exact order taught to me by Silas.

As soon as I finish, I move to the next. That's Bodie, done. Kaden, done. Brooklyn, done.

"Make haste, Mitzy."

Easy for him to say. I grasp Hutton's hand, and as I'm tracing the third symbol, she blinks her black-lined eyes. My heart skips a beat and I have to hold my breath to maintain focus. My finger is drawing down the last ligature of the final symbol when she fully awakens.

"What is your issue? What are you doing to my hand?"

"Nothing. Cool ring." I step back and try to act casual. "You guys better get over to the historical society and get those maps. I'll catch up with you in the dorms later."

Silas opens the door, and the five vaguely confused, slightly foggy Defenders of nothing shuffle out in single file. He closes the door and breathes a sigh of relief. "Impressive. Your focus is expanding daily. And your ability to receive messages is also vastly improved."

I collapse onto one of the visitor chairs and pant, as apprehension drains from my body. "I was so worried. I lost my focus a little at the end. I drew the right symbol, but Hutton was coming around."

Silas places a calming hand on my shoulder and I sense nourishing energy soaking into my being. "You performed the runes exactly as you were taught. There was no mistake, no damage. You removed their memory of this meeting and only this meeting. Now you should rest."

"Yeah, I feel kind of empty."

"I would never ask you to do more than you are capable of, Mizithra."

I stumble across the wind-swept quad toward my Jeep, and the image of curling up under my down comforter with Pyewacket at my side warms me from the inside out.

Unfortunately, once I start the engine, my hands seem to have plans of their own.

For some reason, I'm not afraid, but I'm hoping this isn't Rory's doing.

The next thing I know, I'm turning down a dirt road next to an enormous sign for McClintock's Divine Dairy.

Is this the farm owned by Ainsley's father? Did I know where this was? If I didn't know where it was, how did I get here? Either way, I trust he knows where his daughter is, because I'd hate to be the one to tell him she might've been kidnapped by a deranged practitioner of the dark arts.

The two-story farmhouse bears the typical coat of white paint and has a large screened porch enclosing the entrance. Three huge red barns stand like sentries to the right of the house, and farm implements, too numerous to mention, are strewn about the property.

I approach the front entrance hesitantly and ease the screen door closed behind. Sure, I could let it slam like every screen door in every country song you've ever heard, but I'm not entirely sure why I'm here and I prefer to take a more subtle approach.

There's no doorbell.

However, there is a large metal triangle hanging from a sturdy steel arm. Since I'm not here to call the hired hands to dinner, I'll go with a more traditional option.

Knocking softly at first, and then with increased volume, I wait.

A large man with rough red cheeks and a redder neck answers the door. He smells of earth and hard work, and an unfriendly expression weighs down his features. "We don't support no charities except our own, and I ain't had time to read a magazine since 1975." He begins to push the door closed.

"Mr. McClintock?" It's as good a guess as any. "I'm actually a friend of Ainsley's. We're in the archaeology program together at the community college."

The gap widens an inch or two. "She ain't takin' no visitors, ya know."

A sigh of relief escapes my lips. "She's here? She's all right?"

The door opens a bit farther. "What do you know about it?"

"I know she was working on a special project with Professor Klang before he was killed . . ." I reach into my jacket and slip out the photograph of Ainsley next to the pile of artifacts. "And I think it might've had something to do with this."

The door flies open wide, and he reaches to his right.

Before I can say "got milk," I'm staring down the double-barrel of a shotgun.

"Get off my land. Get back in whatever devil wagon brought you here and don't come back." His finger rests solidly inside the trigger guard. "No one is gonna dig up my farm, and that's final. Now, get!"

Slowly backing toward the screen door, I worry what this man might do to someone who doesn't take no for an answer. I'm not sure what to say to him, but this is my one chance to get a little piece of information. "Mr. McClintock, I don't want to cause any trouble. I'm trying to find out who killed the professor. I'm worried that Ainsley might be in danger, especially if those artifacts are the real deal."

He fires a warning shot past my head, and buck-shot rips through the rusty screen.

I shove the screen door open, let it bang shut for all to hear, and run to my Jeep. The frigid air stings my cheeks and burns my throat, but it's nothing compared to the pain of being shot if I stop running. At some point I drop the photograph, but with the negative safe at the sheriff's station, there's no point risking buckshot in the behind to pick it up.

Diving into my vehicle, I kick up a rooster tail of dust and gravel as I tear out of the Divine Dairy.

And no, the nomenclature-based irony is not lost on me.

CHAPTER 14

IT'S NEVER a good day when someone shoots at you, but, on the upside, Ainsley is safe at home and not being held against her will by Rory Bombay.

I need a decent cup of hot chocolate and an extravagant pastry to help me process all of this information.

Next stop, Bless Choux patisserie on Third Avenue.

The crowd is thinner than expected for the afternoon rush, but the proprietor, Anne, is bustling around as though the line stretches around the corner. When I get my turn at the counter, I order an extra-large Mexican hot chocolate and a chocolate croissant. "You seem awfully busy. You wouldn't happen to have time to teach a girl how to make a pie, would you?"

She chuckles, and her eternal smile shines on me. "I'd be happy to teach you how to make pie eleven months out of the year, Mitzy, but November isn't one of those months. I have orders for pumpkin, pecan, apple, and strawberry rhubarb pies longer than both my arms and legs. And every single one of them has to be baked and boxed by this Wednesday. But I tell you what, if you'd like to place an order, I'm happy to tell everyone you baked it yourself."

Her kind accommodation always surprises me. "I'd like to order a pumpkin. I'm not sure how many people will be there. Is one pie enough?"

She sets my chocolate croissant on a plate and shakes her head playfully. "One pie is never enough. If you're headed out to Twiggy's shindig, you better take a pumpkin and an apple. I happen to know that's her favorite."

My mouth waters at the sight of the croissant. "You know everything that happens in this town, don't you?"

We share a chuckle and I confirm my order for the two pies. "Hey, on the topic of knowing everything, what do you know about the McClintock's and their dairy farm?"

For the first time since I stumbled into her patisserie, the smile on her face fades. "That was some bad business."

My extrasensory antennae tingle with anticipation. "Something bad happened out at the farm?"

She glances at the short line behind me and leans across the counter. "Give me a minute to take care of these folks, and I'll stop by your table."

"No problem." I pay for my snack and my pie order, and take the croissant to a corner table.

A few minutes later, Anne appears with a beautiful mug of Mexican hot chocolate, topped with a healthy portion of whipped cream and a gentle sprinkling of cinnamon.

She sets the mug on the table without spilling a drop and takes the seat opposite. "Mrs. McClintock was attacked when Ainsley was a little more than a year old. They never caught the man responsible. Rumor has it, he was one of the hired hands, and he moved on, as the seasonal workers always do. Poor Clyde found his daughter wandering down the dirt road and came home to find . . . Well, best not talk about it. Mrs. McClintock was in the hospital for almost two weeks. Clyde was never the same. He got real, you know, protective."

"So he shoots at everyone that shows up unannounced?"

Anne claps her hand on the table and leans back, wide-eyed. "You went out to the farm?"

"Ainsley didn't show up at class today, and I wanted to make sure she was all right."

Her broad smile returns and she chuckles as she points to my wig. "Oh, that explains the getup."

"What do you mean?"

"You know how folks talk in a small town. I've heard a story or two about you wearing disguises and going undercover to solve crimes. When you do good, word gets out."

"I'm trying my best to do good, but I'm not having any luck proving Erick's innocence."

Anne reaches across the table and squeezes my hand. "We all know he's innocent, sweetie. You'll figure it out. I have as much faith in you as I do in my great-grandma's *pâte à choux* recipe." She pats my hand and returns to her kitchen.

It's time to bring Erick up to speed. He'll be angry, but it doesn't feel right to keep him in the dark about Rory. I'll grab a dozen doughnuts to soften the blow.

Furious Monkeys is busy tapping and swiping on her phone when I arrive at the sheriff's station.

"Care for a doughnut?"

Shockingly my offer receives real live eye contact. "Set a jelly-filled next to me. I'm only two coconuts from leveling up and can't stop now."

I place a jelly doughnut on top of the stack of reports next to her and make my way to Erick's office. I am not looking forward to running into

Paulsen, but she doesn't seem the type to say no to a doughnut.

"Can I interest you in a doughnut, Deputy?"

"It's Acting Sheriff, and yes." She reaches into the box and grabs a large bear claw.

Now to test the waters with my news. "Hate to be the one to tell you, but I'm pretty sure Rory Bombay is behind Gerhardt Klang's murder. I think he purposely set up Erick to take the fall."

Her mouth is already full, and she chews slowly as my words sink in. She swallows and wipes the crumbs from the corner of her mouth with the back of her hand. "You got any evidence?"

Since I can't really tell her about cursed rune-stones or psychic messages I'm left with a gigantic pile of nothing. "Not yet."

"Well, if it's a setup, it's a good one. The trace came back on that needle today—victim's blood inside. The outside had been wiped clean. I'm afraid we'll have to charge Harper, but I'm gonna keep him in our holding cell as long as I can. County jail is no place for a sheriff. If we don't find something to clear his name before the holidays, my hands will be tied. He'll have to transfer to County and await his trial."

If ever there was a gloomier sentence, I haven't heard it. "I'll find something. I'm sure I'll find something." As I turn to leave the office, she calls out.

"Moon, you shouldn't tell him about Bombay. He's like a powder keg back there, and I'm afraid that name will light the match."

"All right. For now. But if I get you some evidence, you'll— I mean, you know he's innocent, right?"

"My opinion isn't the law. Like I told you before, I have to follow the evidence, just like the sheriff would if he was in my position."

"Copy that." At least there's a hint of apology in her tone. That's something.

The hallway outside the holding cells seems narrower, the paint more disheartening, and the air colder than I remember. Erick gazes toward me as I walk in front of the bars, but his eyes don't light up.

"I brought you doughnuts."

He laughs once. The sound is sharp and hollow. "My last meal, eh?"

Tilting the box, I pass it through the bars and set it softly on the cement floor. "Absolutely not. In fact, it's a celebration."

His eyes dart up, and the weight of his hope threatens to break my heart. "You found something?"

"Yes, but I can only tell you if you promise to remain calm."

He stands and stalks to the bars. "I don't know if I can make that kind of promise, Moon."

"You have to. *Acting Sheriff* Paulsen made me promise not to tell you, but I can't stand seeing you like this."

"Look, they've got my jersey with the vic's blood, the murder weapon from my gear bag, and I've got no alibi. Even if it's more bad news, it's better than nothing, I guess."

"I hope you still feel that way thirty seconds from now." I take a deep breath and ignore the burning ring of fire on my left hand. I'm sure the universe at large is screaming at me to keep my secrets, but when I look into those helpless blue eyes, I'd do anything to change his fate. "It's Rory Bombay."

My extra senses pick up on the building rage, and I step away from the bars. Erick kicks the box of doughnuts, grabs the quilt his mother brought him off the bench, and throws it across the tiny cell. "What has that guy got against me?"

I swallow and whisper, "Me."

His wild, fierce anger vanishes faster than a Sedona sunset. "You? Don't you dare try to take responsibility for that madman."

I step toward the cell and place my hands on the bars. "It's true. If I'd just given him what he wanted." I choke back the tears and try to continue. "He would've never come after you. He would've taken what he wanted from me, picked up his stupid relics from McClintock's farm, and you'd still be sheriff."

Erick exhales loudly and he places his hands lovingly over each of mine. "I still am sheriff. You and I are the best crime-solving team north of the Gulf of Mexico. Let's stop feeling sorry for ourselves and put our giant brains to use."

I lean against the bars and our lips meet in a passionate kiss, as a tear trickles down my cheek.

My mood ring has no time for lovey-dovey nonsense. The heat is so intense it feels as though my ring finger is on fire. I pull my hands away and look down. Ainsley has a gag in her mouth and she's weeping. I don't need to see any more of the image to know that Rory has taken her. My new commitment to honesty is going to have to be shelved.

Erick leans against the bars with concern. "What's wrong? Not to toot my own horn, but usually you don't pull away from a kiss like that."

When in doubt, lie it out. "Yeah, sorry. The kiss was amazing. Something popped into my head . . . I need to talk to Silas." I hold a hand to my head as though the pressure can force a solution to the surface. "Should I send someone in to clean up the doughnuts?"

Erick blushes shamefacedly. "Nah, I'm gonna eat 'em off the floor as penance. That's where I'm at now, Moon. Will you be back today?"

"Let's say by morning. It's a bit of a drive out to Silas's place, and I'm not sure how long it'll take to get the information I need. Do you want breakfast from the diner or the patisserie?"

"How about you surprise me?" A weak smile touches his lips.

I turn and march toward the door, and hear him call after me. "Don't do anything stupid."

The man knows me too well.

There's no time to actually drive out to see Silas. A call will have to do. I put the phone on speaker and drive, hoping for psychic guidance.

"Good afternoon, Miss Moon. How may I be of assistance?"

"Silas, Rory has taken one of the girls as bait. I know he won't hurt her—yet. There's something to those artifacts in that picture of Ainsley. I need your expertise. We have to figure out what he wants and give it to him. I hate to let him get away again, but I don't want anyone's blood on my hands."

"I shall meet you at the bookshop. Bring the photograph."

"Yeah, about that . . ." As I drive back to the Bell, Book & Candle, I bring Silas up to speed on the unholy events at McClintock's Divine Dairy. He assures me that with minor coaching, I should be able to recall every detail of the photograph.

Since there's no time to get Mr. Knudsen to develop another print, my psychically enhanced recall is our best bet.

Twiggy has already left for the day, so I don't have to update her on the Thanksgiving menu change-up. My dad and Amaryllis can bring dinner rolls. I can't believe Twiggy thought I couldn't make a pie. I mean, technically I'm not the one making a pie, but po-tay-to, po-tah-to.

CHAPTER 15

GRAMS BURSTS THROUGH the wall separating the bookshop from the printing museum. "Oh, thank goodness. I was worried sick."

"Why? What happened here?"

"He was here! That snake, Rory Bombay! He couldn't use any of his wily tricks. At least the protections Silas put in place did that much. He tried to steal a book, and Twiggy had to pepper-spray him!"

I shake my head in disbelief. "Good for her. Did he get the book?"

Grams places a ring-ensconced fist on each hip. "You've met Twiggy, right, dear?"

Despite the tension, we both chuckle.

"Silas is on his way over. He'll definitely want

to know which book Rory was after. Do you remember?"

"Of course! I went and made a card and tacked it on the murder wall as soon as Twiggy got rid of that viper."

"Wow! You might need to open your own after-life detective agency."

"Oh Mitzy! You're such a hoot."

A key slips in the lock, and the thick metal door from the alley swings open. I'm not sure I've ever been happier to see Silas.

"Rory was here. He tried to steal a book, and Twiggy gassed him."

Silas calmly slips his key into his jacket pocket, dons his bespelled spectacles, and smooths his mustache with a thumb and forefinger. "Is he dead?"

"I should've been more specific. She pepper-sprayed him. He didn't get the book, but he got away, and now he's got Ainsley."

Taking off my thick winter coat, I toss it on a chair in the back room. "We need to figure out what he wants, get our hands on it, and then set a trap. And this time it needs to be a trap that won't fail."

Silas harrumphs. "Easier spoken than executed. He is a cunning man of many deadly talents, and dark powers. Each time we meet, I fear he grows more powerful. Would you not agree, Isadora?"

Grams nods her translucent head.

I cross my arms over my chest and scoff. "Well, I'm not above killing him." I do my best impression of the classic Robert De Niro nod, in every movie he's ever made. "I have a gun."

"Mizithra!" Silas and Grams remarkably admonish me in unison, even though he can't hear her.

The tears that I carefully kept at bay at the sheriff's station come tumbling out. "They found Klang's blood in the needle on that hand pump thingy. They're charging Erick with murder, today! It's not all right, and I can't handle it. I let myself care for someone and the same thing that always happens, happened again. He's going away. He's going away and he's breaking my heart."

Grams is the first to rush to my side. She slips an ethereal arm around my shoulders and coos softly into my ear. "There, there, dear. Erick isn't abandoning you. A nasty, horrible rat of a man has set up the good sheriff. It's our responsibility to turn the tables."

I translate for Silas.

"Without impugning any additional parties," he adds.

"All right, but I'm just saying." I swipe at my cheeks and pantomime cocking my finger-gun.

"There will be no need for firearms, Mitzy. Let's proceed upstairs and review the evidence. We know far more about this case and the true culprit than Deputy Paulsen."

I snuffle loudly and wipe my nose with the back of my hand. "Yeah. We're the Scooby Gang, and he's the crooked real estate developer."

As I walk toward the spiral staircase, Grams and Silas share a confused shrug.

Not bothering to explain my TV reference, I unhook the "No Admittance" chain and defiantly leave it hanging.

Silas takes his usual place in the scalloped-back chair and I arrange myself comfortably on the settee.

Pyewacket issues a low growl from his perch atop the antique armoire, next to the secret door.

"I hear your complaints, Pye. We're definitely going to get him this time. So if you have any other clues you were saving for a rainy day, today's the day."

"RE-OW!" Game on!

"I couldn't have said it better myself, son." I fold an arm under my head and take a deep breath. "What must I do, all-knowing mentor?"

Silas refuses to take the bait. "The process of psychic recall is delicate. Your opinions can alter the accuracy of your perceptions. You must release all of your preconceived notions and endeavor to describe the items in the photograph exactly as they appear."

"Copy that. No creative license."

Silas steeples his fingers, and as he leans back and slowly bounces his chin, he delivers the instructions. "Close your eyes and clear your mind of distractions. Count down from ten and, after each number, exhale any unwanted thoughts that appear."

I close my eyes and begin the count. "Ten, nine—"

"You may recite the count silently. Picture yourself descending a staircase, and each number represents a step farther down. When you reach the bottom, you'll see a beautiful door. Open it."

The door is magnificent. In fact, it looks very similar to the wooden door at the front of my bookshop. A thick timber slab intricately carved with whimsical vignettes. A centaur chasing a maiden through delicate woodland. A faun playing a flute for a family of rabbits dancing around his cloven feet. The shadow of a winged horse passing in front of the moon. A wildcat stalking a small boy—and the cat bears a striking resemblance to Pyewacket. I reach for the handle and it turns easily.

"Step into the room. In front of you, there is a lavender-colored screen. On this screen you may call up the memory of your choosing."

Staring at the projection screen, I wonder how I've not come to this room before. There are so many things I want to see. Maybe I could call up a memory of my mom.

"Your breathing indicates distraction. Push the other thoughts away. You may return to this room any time you choose. It is your inner world. For today, right here, right now, you must call up the image of the photograph."

It takes a moment to steady my breathing and let go of selfish desires. As soon as I turn my attention to the crisp black-and-white photograph printed for me by Mr. Knudsen, it blooms to life on the screen in front of me, like an inkblot spreading across paper.

"Good. Now, take your time as you examine the image. Start on the left and let your eyes drift over the picture. Each time you see something of interest, describe it to me."

There's little Ainsley, probably about two years old, wearing an adorable floral sundress. "The photo was taken in the summer."

"Excellent. What else do you see?"

I shift my gaze to the pile of artifacts. "There are nails. They look handmade, probably iron. There are some small metal discs; they could be rivets. There's a piece of stone, kind of cone-shaped, but smooshed. It has a wide rounded base and the top is flat, with a hole all the way through. I don't know what that is."

"It's not important for you to know; simply describe things to me. What you're seeing is likely a spindle whorl, most assuredly carved from soapstone. Is there anything else?"

I never realized how soothing Silas's voice could be. My focus drifts and I have to pull it back to the photograph. "Yes, there's a bronze pin. I think it's a cloak pin."

"Very good. Anything else?"

"Yes, a piece of jewelry."

"Excellent. Can you describe it?"

A strange feeling of *otherness* comes over me, and words I've never heard come out of my mouth. "It is the golden torc Brísingamen. Made for the goddess Freya by the dwarven tribes. It holds the power of the sorceress of seiðr. It carries the power to make the wearer irresistible."

Gasping, I'm ripped from the mystical room. I fall back into my body with a frightful thud.

Silas stands and places a hand on my forehead. He mumbles, "Requietio," and I fall asleep.

When I open my eyes, Pyewacket is curled up in the curve of my body and Silas is sipping a cup of tea while an arcane tome lies open in his lap.

"You did wonderfully, Mitzy. Your description of the torc was spot on. Isadora showed me the book

Rory was attempting to steal. It is a hand-written compilation of the rituals of Freya. The power of her gold torc is not to be underestimated. I believe we have stumbled upon the exact thing our nemesis seeks. The question is, where is it now? And how can we see that no harm comes to this Ainsley, and yet preserve the priceless artifact?"

I sit up and rub my eyes. My entire body aches with a grogginess I've never before experienced. "Isn't Freya a mythological figure? I mean, a Norse goddess isn't an actual person, right?"

"Whether the goddess chose to take human form is not our debate. We seek the torc as a means to rescue the girl."

The details of my vision are seeping back in like smoke under a door. "Did I say it makes the wearer irresistible?"

Silas nods affirmatively.

"That sounds about right. I guess Rory figured if he couldn't woo me the old-fashioned way with gifts of cursed jewelry, he'd mesmerize me by wearing a necklace that would make him irresistible. *Dirty Rotten Scoundrels,* part two!"

Pyewacket snarls and Grams nods furiously. "That man has been up to no good for far too many decades. I'm reconsidering your suggestion on guns."

Grams' brazen flip-flopping makes me chuckle, and Silas tilts his head questioningly.

I quickly interpret. "Oh, it's Grams getting on board with my gun idea."

"That will not be necessary. We know he doesn't possess the torc. If he did, he would have no reason to kidnap the girl."

"But how did he get her? Her dad pulled a gun on me ten seconds after I got there, and I wasn't even acting threateningly. Plus, how do we know where this picture of her was even taken? Maybe they were at a friend's house or something."

Silas fixes me with his uber-mentor stare. "How indeed?"

"Oh, right." I close my eyes, take a deep breath and seek the answer. "They definitely took the photograph at the Divine Dairy. We have to get in there and somehow get these artifacts. I mean, technically Clyde shouldn't have them, right? Why do you think he didn't report his findings to someone? This seems like a very important archaeological discovery."

Silas harrumphs. "There is more to Mr. Mc-Clintock than meets the eye. We may need to take the necklace by force."

"Should I get my gun?"

"Settle down, Annie Oakley. We have far more

subtle tools at our disposal." Silas pats his coat of many pockets.

"Should I tell Paulsen about the kidnapping?"

"What evidence do you have to offer other than your vision?"

"Yeah, I see what you did there."

He smiles encouragingly. "Let me finish this passage and transcribe the remainder of my reference notes, and then I believe we shall take a drive out to the heavenly milk house."

"It's Divine Dairy, Silas."

"To be sure."

Grams flits around in a panic, and in her agitated state can't manifest enough corporeal form to open the secret panel underneath one of the built-in bookcases in the apartment.

"Let me get that for you, Grams." I press the panel, and the long wide drawer eases open.

She attempts to dig through the contents, but again her phantom fingers let her down.

"What are you looking for? Tell me. I can find it."

"It's a bracelet. It will protect you from Rory, I think."

"You think a bracelet will protect me? It would be great if you could be more certain."

Silas clears his throat as he approaches the open

drawer. "Alchemy is a blend of science and the supernatural. Science maintains a degree of predictability, while the supernatural is slightly less compliant." He reaches into the drawer, slides over a smudge bundle of sage, and retrieves the copper bracelet. He slips the cuff over my right wrist. "If you feel Mr. Bombay's subtle manipulations swirling toward you, hold the bracelet in front of you and say, 'Ektrépo'."

I press a hand to my chest and stifle a giggle. "Like Wonder Woman? You seriously just gave me a Wonder Woman bracelet?" Hugging the bracelet to my heart, I gaze at the copper cuff and smile. "I love my life!"

Grams swirls through Silas and he steps back with a shiver. "Listen, young lady, this is no joke. That bracelet saved my life, once or twice. Not the last time, but I was sick. That's different. You wear it, and don't get smart."

I stand in the position of attention, with my fists at my sides. "Yes, sir, Major Ghost-ma, sir. Private Moon acknowledges."

My silliness softens her concern, and she chuckles as she drifts toward the ceiling.

"You know your way to this dairy, Mitzy?"

"I do. Let's rock . . . and ride!"

Silas scrunches up his face in confusion, but as I walk toward the Rare Books Loft, he follows without comment. It's the battle cry from *Biker Mice from Mars*, if you were wondering.

Time to save the girl, rescue a priceless mythological artifact, and crush an obsessed sorcerer.

You call it a blockbuster movie; I call it Monday night.

CHAPTER 16

As we bump along the gravel road to McClintock's Divine Dairy, my misgivings about the plan, and concern over potentially getting shot, consume me. "Clyde wasn't in a very generous mood earlier. I'm betting that hasn't improved."

Silas nods and his jowls brush the collar of his shirt. "I would tend to be in agreement, if it weren't for one variable."

"Which is?"

"The disappearance of his daughter. We know that Mr. Bombay shies away from getting any dirt directly on his hands. However, his scheme to force Gerhardt's students to do his bidding with the cursed runestones collapsed in a dead end. Perhaps he attempted to pressure Professor Klang into stealing the remainder of the relics and Klang refused."

"Or Klang planned to double-cross him, and Rory chose to eliminate a traitor."

"A fair point." He nods as he ponders. "A father's love for his daughter is a powerful thing. For some reason, which I cannot grasp, Mr. McClintock watched his daughter be carted away rather than turn over the relics." Silas smooths his mustache and grumbles under his breath.

"You're assuming he had a choice. What if Rory secretly took Ainsley, or took her by magical force, and intends to use her as ransom?"

A heavy dread settles over the car as we make our final approach to the dairy.

In the gloaming, the white farmhouse looms with a sinister vibe.

"What's our next move?"

Silas exhales and cracks his knuckles. "I shall attempt a civil request for entry. If civility is denied, I shall be forced to immobilize Mr. McClintock while we search the property."

"Copy that. Am I waiting in the car for a sign, or do I follow you in now?"

"A valuable query. Since your earlier interaction with the farmer was less than positive, perhaps it would be best if you delay, and await the sign." Silas exits the vehicle and closes the door without indicating what sign I'm waiting for, but hopefully it's a clear one.

A soft yellow glow spills from the two windows to the right of the front door. When Silas knocks, the harsh white porch light flicks on, casting a sharp shadow against the screen.

Mr. McClintock answers the door, gun in hand, and an angry voice cuts through the frosty stillness. "No cops!"

He seems momentarily confused to see a doddering old man on his stoop, but after a brief exchange he aims the gun threateningly.

Silas appears to grow several inches in height, and I can feel the vibration of his deep voice in the soles of my feet.

Mr. McClintock lays down his weapon and steps back.

Silas turns toward the vehicle, snaps his fingers, and a flash of blue light pops in the twilight.

There's no mistaking it. That's the sign. I hop out and hurry to his side.

Mr. McClintock walks like a zombie into the living room.

"Be seated, Mr. McClintock."

The farmer drops into his well-worn recliner and folds his hands in his lap.

Silas turns to me. "It is up to you to find the items we seek. Focus. Breathe. Locate."

"Understood." I take a deep breath, and, I must admit, the multiple dishes of potpourri do little to disguise the underlying bouquet of manure.

Having learned a thing or two about the architecture of homes in almost-Canada, I head straight to the basement. You don't get a lot of basements in Arizona, and the creepiness factor still has a palpable effect.

I pull the string hanging from the single bulb and, as the light creates a circle around me, I clear my mind and reach for the torc.

Nothing.

Moving around the damp, musty cement space, I extend my hands as though I'm playing a game of blind man's bluff.

No messages. No feelings. No pretty pictures in my moody ring.

Clearly, I overestimated the importance of basements. Back on the main floor, I continue my extrasensory search. As I enter the bedroom at the end of the hallway, I'm startled to discover a woman asleep in the bed. I gasp and step back. The snafu blows my focus, and it's all I can do to close the door quietly.

Slipping into the living room, I share my news. "There's someone asleep in the bedroom."

"Perhaps it is Mrs. McClintock. Have you met her?"

"No. I heard a story about her from Anne at the patisserie, but for some reason I thought the woman was no longer with us."

Silas flourishes his hand. "She will continue to sleep. Finish the search. I fear time is running out for Ainsley."

At the sound of his daughter's name, Clyde flinches in his chair. Silas turns and tends to the man. "Remain calm. We are friends. We intend to save your daughter."

Clyde blinks once and slips back into the stupor.

I march up the stairs and search the bedrooms on the upper floor.

Nothing, aside from more cloying potpourri.

As I return to the top of the staircase, a pinching pull touches my chest. I turn and glance up and down the hallway. Finally, the psychic in me connects and my head whips back to see an access panel in the ceiling.

"The attic! Of course."

I have to locate a chair or stool. I find what I'm looking for in what must be Ainsley's room, based on the decor. Lots of pop-star posters, a laptop, and a massive collection of Funko Pop! figurines.

I slide the chair under the opening and pull the handle. As it lowers, an attached ladder is revealed.

Folding it out, I climb up and use the light on my phone to search the space.

It's chokingly dusty. There are creepy-crawlies lurking, and I don't wish to disturb any of them. A hanging spider web catches in my hair and I freak out as I try to get the sticky strands off of me.

In the confusion, I drop my phone. As soon as it hits the floor, it's as though a barrier has been lifted. An invisible rope circles around my heart and pulls me forward.

There's an old metal chest, with wooden bands encompassing it. I kneel and open the chest. Without the aid of a light, I reach in and retrieve a heavy stone box.

There are runes carved in the lid.

I scrape the lid to the side and lean it against the trunk. Grabbing my phone, I illuminate the contents. Inside are all the items from the photograph, plus two smaller pieces that must've been absent from the picture, as was the chalice. There's a woven bag on the left-hand side. I pull it open and the golden gleam of the torc shocks me. I expected an item of such age to be tarnished. The goddess Freya has been watching over her jewelry.

Slipping the phone into my pocket, I reach for the stone lid.

The torc *calls* to me, and part of me yearns, in the worst way, to place it around my neck. As I move the lid closer to the box, a push like opposing magnets shoves the top away from the bottom.

"No. You are not for me." Saying it out loud breaks the trance and the lid drops into place with a stony thud.

I exhale with relief, take a deep breath, and choke on attic dust.

Time to grab this box and get the heck out of Creepytown.

When I return to the main floor, Silas's pinched expression evaporates the moment he sees the box. "You found it?"

"I did. It kind of tried to possess me or something."

"Yes, an item of such power would be eager to be wielded. We must depart with haste. The Mc-Clintock's will be unharmed. The immobilization will wear off in a few minutes."

When we reach the paved road, I hesitate and turn to Silas. "Where am I going?"

He calmly replies, "Where is Ainsley being held?"

"I don't know. The image showed her face and the gag in her mouth. That was it." I shrug and rub the steering wheel.

Silas harrumphs and exhales patiently. "Close your eyes and recall the image."

When he answers a question with a question, it

always means a lesson is right around the corner. I should've seen this coming. That's on me.

Taking a deep breath, I do as I'm told. The visual of the fear in Ainsley's eyes is hard to ignore, but I have to look past it. I have to search the edges of the image and find something that— "Pipes! Freezers!"

Silas nods. "And what does this tell you?"

"Rory has her at the ice rink. I saw the pipes from the hydrotherapy whirlpools and the coolers with all the blocks of ice. She's in the locker room. The Abominables' locker room."

"Very well. Drive on."

I wouldn't have said no to a little fanfare, perhaps some overzealous praise, but that's not my mentor's way. I turn onto the paved road and proceed to the fieldhouse. As we approach, I turn off my headlights and pull to the side of the road. "I'm going in alone."

Silas inhales sharply.

"Don't argue with me. I've got this bracelet, and I've dealt with Rory before. You keep the torc and go for backup. I don't care what you have to tell *Acting Sheriff* Paulsen or what spells, I mean, transmutations, you have to perform. You get her and some deputies over here as fast as you can. I can keep Rory talking, but don't leave me tap dancing too long."

Silas grumbles indiscernibly. "I do not care for this plan, Mitzy."

"Neither do I, but it's all we've got. I'm going in, and I'm counting on you to make sure I come back out."

I exit the Jeep and leave the door open.

Silas comes around to the driver's side and places a comforting hand on my shoulder. "Do not let him in. Do not entertain any of his fanciful attempts to control you. Use your gifts, use the bracelet, and remember *everything* I've taught you."

There's a strange hum to the word everything and my skin buzzes with a knowing I can't ignore.

"Copy that. See you on the other side, Willoughby."

He shakes his head, and his jowls waggle as he climbs into the driver's seat. The door slams, and I stoop as I slink into the darkness encompassing the venue.

I've seen enough action films to know that it's important to stay low and move in the shadows. As I inch my way toward the rear entrance of the ice rink, the taillights of the Jeep disappear into the night.

My courage wavers as I face the truth: I truly am alone.

Hopefully, Silas can work his alchemical wizardry on Paulsen and get back here with a posse before Rory gets the best of me.

With my hand resting on the door handle, I run through a few scenarios and whisper softly to the blackness, "No matter what, Ainsley makes it out alive."

Whatever forces linger beyond the veil, I hope they've heard my plea and take it seriously.

CHAPTER 17

THE DOOR IS UNLOCKED, as I'd hoped. More than likely Rory is expecting Clyde McClintock to show up with the torc, in exchange for his daughter. He's probably got the back door under surveillance, so it's best to proceed as though he's watching me right now.

Regardless, I continue to move as stealthily as my natural clumsiness will allow. Rather than draw unnecessary attention with the light from my phone, I move cautiously in the dim red glow of the "EXIT" signs.

As I approach the Abominables' locker room, an eerie chuckle reverberates through the arena.

"How perfect. I should've known you would come to that Boy Scout's defense."

The best defense is a good offense. I'm sure I heard that somewhere. No point letting Rory know that I have any doubts about my ability to succeed this evening. "First of all, Erick isn't a Boy Scout. And I'm not here to defend him. I'm here to take Ainsley home to her family, and you better not get in my way."

He laughs out loud and steps from the shadows. "Your concern for others will be your downfall, Mitzy."

I twist the handle of the locker room door. Pulling it open, I dash inside. He'll surely follow, but if I can get to Ainsley, maybe I can offer her a moment of reassurance.

As I round the corner her terrified eyes meet mine and shift from surprise to confusion. I rip the gag out of her mouth and, shockingly, the first thing she says is, "Darcy, what did you do to your hair?"

Oops. I kind of forgot that I wasn't wearing the wig on this mission. "It's a long story, Ainsley. I'm going to get you out of here, all right? I need you to do exactly what I say. No questions asked. Got it?" The smell of fear hangs in the air.

The thud of Rory's boots on the cement floor echoes in the empty locker room. "She loves to be in control, Ainsley. She's very much about people doing exactly what she says." He snarls under his breath. "I hate to be the one to burst your bubble, Mitzy, but if you didn't bring me the torc, neither of you are leaving this locker room alive."

The panic rushes back into Ainsley's eyes and her mermaid-green bangs fall across her face as she cowers against the metal therapy tub.

I turn to face him, and even in the dim lighting, his green eyes sparkle with malice. "That's not how this is going to end, Frank. You're not getting the torc. Mr. McClintock isn't coming. In fact, he no longer has the item you seek." I choose to use his childhood name in a feeble hope that stabbing beneath his "Rory Bombay" façade, to the real Frank Freeman, might throw him off.

My extra senses pick up on a flash of surprise and a soupçon of fear, but Rory quickly adjusts his attack.

I feel the tingle in the air that I've come to recognize as his singular brand of manipulative magic. I raise the copper bracelet over my chest and hold the word "Ektrépo" firmly in my mind.

The venom in his eyes shifts to shock, followed by desire, as he stares at the bracelet and lusts to possess it.

I lift my chin and press on. "Toss me the key to her handcuffs. If you cooperate, I'll let you walk out of here."

He scoffs and squares his shoulders. "Your natural talents are still amateurish, and no match for my skills. I have studied texts that you and your bookshop merely dream of owning. If that wannabe druid Silas Willoughby has the torc, he will deliver it, or he will lose his last apprentice." The edge of hatred in Rory's voice cuts through the air like a knife.

I'm not sure what I expected, but I had no idea he would be willing to kill me to get what he wanted. So much for thinking I was the prize. Clearly, I'm simply another meaningless pawn in his great game. New plan. "You know Silas better than I do. He won't negotiate with you. I'm sure he'd rather not have me killed for no reason, but he certainly won't hand you a powerful relic in exchange for my life. He may care for me, but he'll weigh one life against the greater good. You know he can't be manipulated."

"We shall soon find out." And like a cobra striking, he lunges for me. Ripping the bracelet from my wrist, in its place he loudly clicks a handcuff. Rory yanks me toward the pipe and claps the other end around it.

I twist my wrist in the cuff and glare at him. At least I still have my mobile.

"Before you get any bright ideas, I'll be taking

this." He pulls my phone from my back pocket and smirks as I sink to the floor next to Ainsley.

"This isn't over."

He sneers and turns his back to me. "Let me place a quick call and put your theories about Silas Willoughby to the test." He dials and utters a single phrase. "Bring me the torc or they both die."

Ainsley begins to cry.

Ignoring the young girl's whimpering, I slide my handcuff up the pipe and get to my feet. "Why Klang? Was it random, or did you have a score to settle with him?"

Rory smashes my phone against the cement floor, cracks his knuckles, and grins. "It is dangerous to disappoint me. As you well know."

I roll my eyes.

"Gerhardt Klang was one of the most promising archaeologists to enter the scene in decades. I was certain I could manipulate his passion for history into a lucrative stream of artifacts for my network of collectors. If he happened to uncover anything of magical significance, all the better for me." He bows as though accepting a standing ovation.

"Was this partnership voluntary, or did you control him with a cursed object as well?"

Rory's throaty, devilish chuckle makes the hair on my arms stand on end.

"In the beginning it was voluntary. He was desperate for funding for his research, and I was happy to accommodate him. However, when he got mixed up in the Kensington Runestone debacle, he lost his prestigious appointment at Durham, and I lost a powerful rook in my game."

"So why not find another desperate nerd to control?"

"Tsk tsk. You reveal so much of your naïveté with these questions, Miss Moon. The subtle magicks that bend others to your will are difficult to maintain. A willing participant is far more valuable than one such as yourself."

The harsh tone in his voice forces me to swallow uncomfortably, but I have to keep him talking. "So you followed him back to Birch County and renewed your partnership?"

He shrugs. "In a manner of speaking. Our falling out was financially disruptive to my business, and he suspected my hand in the blacklisting that followed his disgrace. He was none too eager to do me any favors." Rory runs a hand through his jet-black hair and sighs. "Then I discovered his little group of fawning minions. What better way to influence the puppet master than to possess his puppets? I insisted Gerhardt call a meeting of his so-called Defenders to announce my financial backing of their yet-to-be-approved dig, and I passed out the runestones as valuable tokens, binding them to glory and riches when the treasures were uncovered."

Ainsley's sobbing subsides, and she leans toward her captor. "Special-K didn't want to sell the artifacts. He wanted us to publish a scholarly paper and have an exhibit." She chokes and sniffles. "He didn't want the money. He wanted vindication."

Rory crouches beside her. "You are as foolish as you are trusting. Gerhardt Klang was no more in love with you than I. His manipulations may have led to a different reward than mine, but both of us wanted the artifacts—and nothing more."

Ainsley's weeping resumes.

My psychic senses feel an added layer of broken heartedness in this new wave of sorrow. "Why kill him? If you both had the same goals . . . Why the murder?"

He steps a hand's breadth from me and stares down into my eyes. "He wanted to change the rules. No one changes the rules but me."

I shudder and step away. "And Erick? Did you frame him just to hurt me?"

Rory strides away, laughing uproariously. The fact that his humorous outburst is mostly a performance does not escape me.

"Serendipity, my dear. I attended that broomball game with the sole purpose of putting an end to Gerhardt's life. When I observed the brutality on the ice, the plan simply unfolded before me."

"But the air pump? Erick drove his cruiser to the lake. How did you plant that evidence?"

"Ah, yes. That twist was not predicted. I assumed he would drive you home and celebrate his win like a real man. I had no idea he'd sink into introspection and wander off to sulk in solitude. In fact, I was late to my meeting at the fieldhouse with Klang because of the added delay of driving out to the lake. Luckily, your precious sheriff had passed out in a drunken stupor. I had more than enough time to finish off Klang and replace the hand pump."

"You'll never get away with—"

"I already have."

I wish I could slap that smug grin right off his face.

"Enough banter. I need to place some *sentries* around the perimeter." He winks at me and continues, "You two girls get acquainted. I'll be back before you know it. Try not to miss me too desperately, Mizithra."

Oh, it's on. He knows I prefer Mitzy. Well, two can play that game. "No problem, *Frank*. Take your time."

He leaves to set what I'm sure are a series of magical traps, which will alert him to the arrival of any intruders, and his throaty chuckle lingers behind him, making my skin crawl and my stomach churn.

When the locker room door clicks shut, I breathe a sigh of relief.

"Ainsley, we have to hurry. Listen to me carefully and don't ask any questions. There's no time. I'll explain everything later, once I'm sure you're safe."

She whimpers. "Who are you? Why does he keep calling you Mitzy?"

"No questions, remember?"

She sobs and gasps for breath. "Okay. Okay. Please don't let that creepy guy kill me."

"Copy that."

If I have any chance of keeping my promise to Ainsley, I need to work fast. I close my eyes and place my free hand over the lock securing the cuff around my wrist. Using the transmutation that Silas taught me the first time we were in a holding cell together, I picture ice changing state from solid to liquid. I can feel the mechanism release inside the lock.

Pulling my hand free, I grip the lock on Ainsley's cuff next.

"What are you doing? You know how to pick locks?"

It's pointless to keep reminding her not to ask questions. The best approach seems to be to simply ignore her.

The lock releases and she rubs her red wrist as she clutches it to her chest. "What if he comes back?"

"I'm counting on that." I place a hand on either side of her face. "Ainsley, look at me."

Her big brown eyes stare up at me, and her bottom lip quivers.

"I want you to go sit on that bench and cry. When he comes through the door, you tell him I broke free and left you behind. You cry, you scream, whatever you have to do. Make sure he doesn't take his eyes off you."

She shakes her head. "I can't do it. What if— What about you? Where will you be?"

"Look, kid, the less you know the better. If you want to get out of here alive, you do what I say. Now get on that bench and cry your eyes out—like your life depends on it."

She hugs her arms around herself, sits on the bench and rocks back and forth as she sobs.

It's definitely not an act. I reach out with all of my senses, searching for anything that I can use as a weapon.

The equipment is locked up. There's no time to . . . and then—

The smiling cartoon polar bear.

"The 'C' was missing! CHILLY BEAR. Pyewacket, I love you." I open the door of the freezer and grab a ten-pound block of solid ice by its plastic-bag handle.

Pressing myself against the wall next to the door, I ready my arm, like a catapult, and wait for Frank Freeman, a.k.a. Rory Bombay, to return.

He chuckles wickedly as he pushes open the door. "Help has not arrived, gir—" He stops with one hand still on the doorknob.

One thin metal door separates us. I hold my breath.

"How did you get out of your handcuffs? Where's Mitzy?"

Ainsley screams, and when he steps forward, I swing the block of ice with all my might.

It connects solidly with the side of his skull. He teeters and falls like a tree in the forest.

I've never been able to grasp the purpose of the random philosophical thought experiment, "If a tree falls in a forest and no one is around to hear it, does it make a sound?"

But today it all makes sense, and someone is here, and someone hears it. And I couldn't be more pleased.

"Ainsley, run."

For once, she doesn't ask any questions. She races out of the locker room like a jackrabbit with a coyote on its tail, and the door slams behind her with the ominous clang of a portcullis.

I am alone. No help has arrived.

All at once the word *everything* rings in my head, and my entire body buzzes with a purpose.

The reversal runes.

I have to use them.

I have to make him forget he ever knew me.

It's the only way to protect the people I love.

Crouching with one knee squarely in the center of his back, I place my finger on his cheek.

My heart is beating so fast. I'm worried I'll never find the focus I need.

The thing that pops into my head is Pyewacket. *Mr. Cuddlekins, you gave me the weapon, now help me get the win. I need to focus. I need to calm down.*

And for a moment I can feel the coarse fur of his back under my hand. The vibration of his purring soothes my chest.

I close my eyes and trace the first symbol on Rory's cheek as I hold the image of our initial meeting at Myrtle's Diner. Simple, casual, no sign of the havoc it would unleash. As I draw the next symbol, I pull up additional memories, and with the third symbol I witness a montage of images displaying his vendetta against Erick.

A deep calm settles over me when I lift my finger to begin the fourth and final symbol.

The locker room door bursts open and Deputy Paulsen, gun drawn, shouts at the top of her lungs, "Hands in the air. Nobody move."

CHAPTER 18

MY HANDS INSTINCTUALLY FLY UP, and the final symbol is left undone.

Rory groans beneath my weight, and strong arms pull me to my feet.

"Erick?" I stare in disbelief. "What are you doing out of jail?"

He hugs me protectively, while Paulsen slaps the cuffs on Rory.

Silas observes from the hallway, a somber expression pulling his hangdog jowls lower than usual. He must see the fear in my eyes. He steps forward as Paulsen pulls Rory to his feet. "Mizithra, you are quite pale. Is everything all right?"

I shake my head.

Rory regains consciousness and scans the faces in the room. "What's going on? Where am I?"

Silas tilts his head ever so slightly, and every fiber of my being knows the question in his eyes.

I shake my head again and struggle to swallow.

Paulsen jerks him roughly toward the door. "Rory Bombay, I'm placing you under arrest on suspicion of murder—"

"Who's Rory Bombay? I'm Frank Freeman." He tugs against the cuffs. "Frank Freeman. I live at 718 Thornwood Ave. I grew up around here. I went to Pin Cherry Harbor High School. Don't you recognize me?"

Paulsen pushes him toward two waiting deputies. "Take him down to the station and process him. Rory Bombay, Frank Freeman, whatever he wants to be called today. Put him under arrest and list all the names." She turns to me and rests her right hand on the handle of her holstered gun. "You'll need to come in and make a statement." Her eyes dart from Erick to me and back. "Sooner, rather than later."

Sheriff Harper tightens his arm around my shoulders. "10-4, Deputy."

Paulsen licks her lips and shakes her head, but she waddles off without another word.

I shrug and turn toward my mentor.

Silas nods silently, and I feel his acceptance. It may not have been exactly what he intended when he told me to use everything he taught me, but I sense no remorse on his part.

Erick hugs me close and kisses the top of my head.

I inhale his woodsy-citrus scent and lean into his chest. "Thanks for coming to my rescue."

He laughs dryly. "If you say so. How exactly did you knock him out?"

I point to the block of ice melting on the cement floor to our left. "Same way he knocked out Gerhardt Klang. A nice flat block of ice that would perfectly mimic Klang's earlier injury on the ice rink."

Erick leans back and looks down at me with admiration. "One of your hunches?"

Shaking my head, I give credit where credit is due. "Actually, you can thank Pyewacket for that tip."

"You and that cat. Someday, you're going to tell me what the two of you are really up to, right?"

I shrug and paint my features as the portrait of innocence.

His well-educated gaze scans the room. "Two pairs of handcuffs. Are you planning on telling me how you got out of those?"

"I pick locks. You know that."

"Mmhmm. And what were you doing kneeling on Frank Freeman? You told me you had a thing for bad boys, but I thought you'd gotten over him. It looked like you were touching his face when we came in. Do I get to hear that explanation?"

Uh oh. Think. Think. "I was checking for a pulse. I hit him pretty hard. I was worried that I might've actually killed him, you know?"

Erick loosens his hold and lets his hands slide down to my waist. "You remember when I mentioned you had a *tell*?"

I nod slowly, attempting to ignore the knot tightening in my stomach.

"Yeah, you've still got it. I think we're getting to the point in our relationship where we don't have so many secrets, Moon. Being honest with each other is an important part of moving forward, don't you think?"

"You're not wrong."

"And you're dodging." He pulls me closer. "It's been a long day. You look exhausted. Please, don't take that the wrong way." He grins apologetically. "Let me take you home. Paulsen can clean up this mess."

I swallow my secrets as surreptitiously as possible, and smile and nod. "I can drive. Give me a chance to freshen up, and then you can check in on me."

Erick gives me a squeeze. "If you insist."

As we pass by Silas in the hall, his hand brushes my shoulder. A wave of something very close to approval passes between us. I hope he's telling me he understands that I didn't do what I did on purpose. I mean, I fully intended to complete the series of runes properly and only remove the memories pertaining to Erick and me. But the interruption resulted in a wipe of a much larger swath of memory than I ever meant to erase.

If Frank Freeman was being honest, it seems that I erased everything that occurred from the moment he changed his name and assumed the identity of Rory Bombay.

Perhaps it's for the best. If Rory's obsession with arcane knowledge and dark magic is what drove him to murder, and manipulate others to murder, maybe we're all better off with a "Rory-free" Frank Freeman.

I hope the nauseous feeling in my stomach indicates my conscience is intact. I have no intention of using my powers for anything but good.

As we meander back to the bookshop, the burden of what might've been, what is, and what could come to pass rests heavily on my young shoulders.

In response to the unspoken weight of my world, Silas harrumphs. "You did what had to be done. The right path is not always the simple path. You saved a life and potentially prevented the suffering of many more."

My grip tightens on the steering wheel. "I guess. It's that *potentially* part that's tripping me up." I draw a shaky breath and continue. "I intended to trace all the runes properly. I held my focus on the reversal of his memories of me, and his negative feelings toward Erick. But Paulsen barged in—"

"You owe me no explanation, Mizithra. And, furthermore, let your conscience be clean. Your intentions were pure, and the universe intervened. The growing darkness within Rory Bombay was far too dangerous to be left to its own devices. This Frank Freeman may be the solution that our little corner of the world needs right now."

Silence settles over us again and my mind spins off to the possibilities Frank Freeman might bring to bear. "He'll still be charged with Klang's murder, right? I mean, regardless of what name he was using at the time, he is the one who killed the professor."

"I fear there is good news and bad news on that front. Deputy Paulsen pulled a partial print from the trunk of Erick's cruiser, which matched the prints they had on file from Rory's previous arrest."

"I'll go out on a limb and say that's the good news."

He nods. "On the matter of standing trial, this rift in Frank's psyche may push his defense toward an insanity plea."

"So you don't think he'll go to jail? He'll get to sit in a nut house somewhere eating tapioca pudding and playing checkers?"

Silas rests his hands in his lap and takes a deep breath. "You say that as though it is a reward."

"Good point." I turn down the alley, pull into the garage, and Silas and I exit the Jeep in silence.

He stops beside the alley door and places a fatherly hand on my shoulder. "Your powers are indeed growing. I am most pleased to see that your concern for others and your capacity for love is expanding at an equal rate."

Despite his high standards of etiquette, I throw my arms around his neck and cry a few tears into his fusty coat. "Thank you for being my moral compass. I couldn't have asked for a better guide." I wipe a finger under each eye. "Now, I need to scrub all this drama off, change into some clean clothes, and get ready to entertain a gentleman caller."

Silas laughs until his cheeks turn cherry red in the glow of the streetlights. "I look forward to spending Thanksgiving with you and the rest of Twiggy's band of misfits."

I pause with the key in the lock. "Wait. Band? Who else is invited?"

"Oh, Twiggy's been quite busy. From what I was able to gather, in addition to the two of us, she's invited her on-again/off-again special friend,

Wayne, and invitations were also extended to your father, Amaryllis, Erick, his mother, and Odell. I believe that is the entire roster."

"Wow! I'm glad I ordered two pies. I mean, I'm glad I'm going to make two pies." I wink at Silas and he chuckles. "What about you know who?" I point to the ghost lurking inside.

"I must bid you adieu, but I wish you the best of luck with that endeavor." He nods politely as he strolls toward his Model T parked on First Avenue.

CHAPTER 19

THE FIRST ENTITY TO greet me when I open the door is Robin Pyewacket Goodfellow.

"Greetings, wise and furry one. Once again, I will have to award you the title of 'Most Valuable Player' on the investigative team. You were one hundred percent right about the devious Rory Bombay pulling the strings of this entire scheme, and you correctly identified the use of CHILLY BEAR ice in the murder plot. Rory used the ice to knock out Klang and then loaded him into the laundry cart, on top of all the towels and jerseys, where he injected the bubble of air, and, finally, dumped the professor at the service entrance. Klang was a big boy, and, while Rory is crafty, he's not strong enough to carry a man that size all the way from the locker room."

"Ree-ow." Soft but condescending.

"Yes, I've already acknowledged your massive intelligence. Now, where's our ghost?"

Before Pye has a chance to share his intel, Ghost-ma blinks into being.

Her shimmering arms encircle me. "You're alive! I knew you could get the best of that serpent."

I return the hug and play the pity card. "I'm sorry I caused you any worry, Grams. Can we postpone the debrief? I could use a hot shower."

She pulls away and looks me up and down. "Go ahead, try *not* to think it."

And like a hypnotist's suggestion, my reunion plans with Erick flood into my mind.

Grams giggles. "Oh my! Let's keep it PG, Mizithra."

A frustrated huff escapes as I stomp up the circular stairs. "I'm taking a shower. Then I'm hanging out with a friend in my apartment. I forbid all ghostly intrusions until noon tomorrow." It's none of her business, but I'm not *planning* on having Erick spend the night. I simply want to leave the window open to possibilities.

She swirls around me grinning ghoulishly. "Noon tomorrow? My, my. Don't count your chickens before they hatch, dear." She continues to snicker.

Without acknowledging her taunt, I walk into

the sacred closet and grab her vintage Oscar de la Renta silver-sequin halter gown.

"Mitzy, what are you doing?" She flickers with panic.

I lay the treasure on the floor and raise my foot above its glimmering folds.

"Don't you— You wouldn't!"

"Noon. Tomorrow." I flick one finger toward the exit.

She whooshes out of the apartment grumbling something about an unnecessary tantrum.

Even a ghost has its vulnerabilities. I carefully pick up the gown and return it to the closet. There's no need for her to know that I would never follow through on my fashion threats.

By the time the telltale "BING BONG BING" of the alleyway bell sounds, I'm fresh as a daisy and fully dressed. In jeans and stuff, nothing daring, in case you were wondering.

As I approach the side door, I trip on absolutely nothing and all my cool vibes vanish in an instant. I take a moment and try to recover some semblance of allure as I push open the door. "Good evening, Sheriff."

He takes my hand, bows deeply, and kisses the curve of my fingers. "I come bearing tidings of gratitude for the Dame Mitzy Moon."

Pulling my hand back as though a bee has stung

it, I giggle and blush. "Who? What are you talking about?"

He stands and avoids my gaze. "It's freezing out here. How about you let me come in, and I'll explain?"

I step back and wave him through. "All right, fess up."

His eyes sparkle with mischief, and his gentle chuckle warms my heart. "I had to look it up on the internet. Since you were my knight in shining armor this time, I wanted to present an appropriate speech, but I wasn't sure what they called 'lady knights.' Apparently, they're called 'dames.' Go figure."

"Thanks, but you were never a damsel in distress."

He exhales and runs his fingers through his long loose bangs. They fall enticingly over his eye, and I'm happy to see he's operating pomade-free this evening. "If you say so."

"Come on up. I have snacks."

He gestures chivalrously. "After you."

When we enter the apartment, I catch sight of the murder wall and hurry to roll it away.

He catches my elbow. "No, no. Leave it. I really want to see how the mind of Mitzy Moon works."

I have no intention of telling him how little of

my mind is on that board. I'll let him draw his own conclusions.

He paces in front of the board and runs his finger along the green yarn connections. "I'm a little surprised to see my name up here. I thought you were trying to prove my innocence?"

"You were connected to the victim. You know that no one can be ruled out—until they are."

He turns and strides toward me.

My tummy flip-flops when I catch sight of the look in his eye.

"You really did save my bacon. If you hadn't brought in that second pathologist and discovered the true cause of death, the investigation would've stalled out."

"But the cause of death made you look even more guilty!"

"I don't disagree." He turns and glances at the board. "But somehow, you followed that trail of twists and lies to Rory Bombay." He pulls me close and leans down to whisper in my ear. "What do I have to do to make you reveal your methods?"

And . . . I'm dead. My heart has stopped beating, I can't breathe, and my knees are jelly. What does he have to do? It's done. His interrogation techniques are irresistible.

His strong arms embrace me and keep me from

collapsing into a puddle on the floor. "You okay, Moon?"

After pulling some air into my lungs, I recover my defensive wit. "You're not gonna break this witness, Harper." I disengage myself and head for the sofa. "Can I interest you in a sweet or savory nibble?"

A heart-melting grin spreads across his face and he joins me on the couch. "I got an unexpected invitation while I was in the slammer." He holds up a finger to put my snarky comment on hold. "Somehow, me and my mom got invited to Twiggy's Thanksgiving potluck. Was that you're doing?"

I shrug. "Maybe. Indirectly. My dad asked me about my plans, and I haven't had any plans since my mom—you know."

He squeezes my hand and nods. "I know."

"I ran the question past Twiggy, and the next thing you know she's invited everyone to her place. Which is great. It's not like I have a kitchen." Nervous laughter tightens my throat, and he smiles wickedly.

"I was wondering about that. Can you cook?"

I pull my hand away and cross my arms. "Depends what you mean by cook. Can I boil water? Yes. Can I heat absolutely anything in my microwave without alerting the fire department?

Pretty much. Can I make duck à l'orange served on a pillow of nutmeg air? Not on your life."

He chuckles and grabs a handful of pretzels.

Pyewacket saunters in and circles the settee expectantly.

"Hey, I understand I owe you a big thanks for the tip about the Chilly Bear ice, big guy." Erick grins and tips his head toward Pye in that way that insinuates he's doffing a cap.

Pye stops, flops onto the Persian rug, and cleans his left paw.

"Would a box of Fruity Puffs be an acceptable tribute?"

The caracal's tail flicks once, and he squeezes his eyes as he gazes at Erick. "Reow." Can confirm.

I open my mouth to translate, but Erick beats me to the punch. "Understood, buddy. I got your back."

Mr. Cuddlekins turns his narrow gaze on me and tilts his head.

I toss him a cheesy puff, and he catches it with one agile paw, clamps it in his fangs, and stalks off to the closet.

The night slips away like sand through an hourglass as we discuss Thanksgiving memories, the importance of family, and canoodle on the couch.

It's nearly 3:00 in the morning when the conversation vanishes and the canoodling takes center stage.

My extra senses flash a warning light and we're clearly approaching the tipping point. I gently disengage. "I'm gonna grab a drink of water. You need anything?"

The heat in his eyes is more answer than I can handle.

As I rush into the powder room to splash some cold water on my face, Erick checks the time on his phone. "Wow, I didn't realize it was so late. I should probably go."

My heart is screaming, *No, don't go. You can stay.* But my new, levelheaded brain is saying, *Take it slow. You're worth the wait.* I return and smile. "Yeah, time got away from us. Breakfast at the diner?"

He shakes his head with regret. "I wish. I'll be eating stale doughnuts at my desk. Paulsen is a great deputy, but she really sucks at administration. I have a mountain of paperwork to catch up on before the holiday, plus I have to prep for the interrogations." He flashes me a half grin. "Mom and I will definitely see you at Twiggy's, though. Sound good?"

Sounds terrible. Sounds like the abrupt ending to a perfect evening, and an entire day moping around on my own. Boo. Hiss. Of course, I don't say any of that to him. "Sounds good. I totally under-stand. I'll walk you out."

When the bookcase door slides open, Pyewacket emerges from the closet and meows in a tone I don't recognize. It's almost like he's asking me what went wrong. Silly cat, don't judge me. I'll deal with you later.

As we're circling down toward the stacks, a happy distraction pops into my head. "By the way, I can't wait to observe the Frank Freeman interroga-tion tomorrow."

He shakes his head in defeat. "I'm not going to waste my breath. That's not an official invite. Not that you've ever needed one."

Before Erick braves the frosty air outside, he pulls me close and kisses me too well and for too long. These trembly legs are never going to make it back up the stairs.

"I'll text you tomorrow, with the interrogation info. Sleep tight, Moon." He glides his hand along the side of my cheek as he exits.

My skin is on fire. My heart is thumping like it ran a marathon. That man will be the death of me, but oh, what a way to go!

I lock the deadbolt and set the alarm.

Maybe if I'm especially good, and the universe is feeling generous, I'll see Sheriff Too-Hot-To-Handle in dreamland.

CHAPTER 20

LUCKILY, I closed the blackout shades earlier this morning before I collapsed into bed, and Grams keeps her word and steers clear of the apartment. So, it is my distinct pleasure to wake up to a late-morning text from Erick.

"Freeman interview in 20."

Yeesh! Time to get crackin'. I hit the button and the shades roll up to reveal a thick layer of swollen grey clouds.

Maybe I should take this whole storm thing more seriously?

I give Pye a good scratch between the ears and roll out of the rack.

Splashes of cold water, a quick pass with a hairbrush, and a last minute swipe of lip tint.

The reflection in the mirror shrugs. "Good enough."

"You're much better than good enough, dear." Grams gestures to the large four-poster bed. "I see you're alone. Did things not go as you planned?" Her perfectly drawn brow arches.

"Erick left around 3:00, which is fine. Things are moving at the exact right pace."

She clutches her pearls and swoons comically. "You're a stronger woman than me!"

"Grams!" I shake my head and march into the closet. "I could use a little moral support."

"You've come to the wrong ghost if you're looking for morals."

We share an eye-watering laugh as I scamper into my clothes.

"I'm off to the station to make sure Rory Bombay is truly 'no more.'"

"Good riddance!" Her eyes widen. "To him, not you, sweetie."

"Copy that."

Since the partial print that Deputy Paulsen recovered from the trunk lid of Erick's cruiser is a match for Frank Freeman's middle finger on his left hand, and the guy kidnapped a couple of people and threatened to kill them, all charges against

Erick have been dropped and he's back on the case.

As I sit quietly in the observation room, sandwiched between Interrogation Rooms One and Two at the sheriff station, I stare through the one-way glass at Frank Freeman.

I've tried every trick in the book. I've reached out with my array of psychic senses, searching high and low for any sign of Rory Bombay. I've held back and quietly waited for extrasensory messages to be delivered as Erick pursues various lines of questioning with Mr. Freeman.

Absolutely no trace of the person calling himself Rory Bombay remains. Every memory that Frank Freeman possesses, of persons or events, are all things that occurred prior to the date he changed his name, over thirty years ago. He has no memory of purchasing Gershon Antiquities (now Bombay Antiquities and Artifacts) in Grand Falls, and he does not understand why he's being questioned in connection to the murder of Gerhardt Klang.

A consummate actor like Rory Bombay could likely fool even a seasoned interrogator like Erick. But under no circumstances would he have the skill to avoid all of my psychic powers. Whatever happened in that moment when Deputy Paulsen interrupted the reversal runes has permanently deleted Rory Bombay.

I wish I could say I feel regret, but I don't. Rory Bombay was a selfish, manipulative, dangerous man. The residents of Pin Cherry Harbor are better off without him. Not to mention, my life and my future look a lot brighter without the specter of Mr. Bombay looming over my shoulder.

Erick completes his questioning and asks Deputy Johnson to prepare the lineup and bring in the witness.

Witness? He didn't mention anyone to me. Does he mean Ainsley? I thought she was still in the hospital for observation.

With my curiosity piqued, I lean forward and await the arrival of the mystery witness.

A few minutes later, Deputy Johnson escorts Kaden Soder into Interrogation Room One.

I crack my knuckles and grin. The speaker is still on from the previous questioning, but I pull my chair closer to the glass. This oughta be rich.

Deputy Johnson leads the sullen sophomore to the chair opposite Erick. The wiry, dark-haired boy drops and arranges his body in a carefully constructed pose intended to send the message that he doesn't care. However, my extra senses can confirm otherwise.

Erick rolls through the basics and Kaden Soder mumbles his replies.

"Look, son, we got an online chat history between you and Ainsley McClintock that puts you in line for an accessory to murder charge and possibly even conspiracy to kidnap. You better sit up and answer my questions like your freedom depends on it." Erick crosses his arms and lifts his chin.

I'm running through the list of charges in my mind and things don't add up. There's absolutely no way Kaden had anything to do with the murder, and I don't think conspiracy to kidnap is even a real charge. Kudos to Erick, for picking up on some of my techniques.

Shockingly, Kaden complies.

"What was your relationship with Ainsley McClintock?"

He scoffs. "She was like a total online stalker. We played this dinosaur game on the same server, you know? A lotta people play. It's not like she was special."

"Seems like she was special enough for you to invite her to join your private Jangle server, and continue the chat outside the game world. What was the purpose behind that?"

Massive eye roll. "She was bragging about some artifacts. I told my professor—"

"This would be Professor Gerhardt Klang?"

"Yeah, Klang. So, I told him some stuff she said, and he was super into it."

Erick nods. "And then?"

"He wanted me to get her to MIRL and bring me the whale horn thing she had."

Erick exhales and uncrosses his arms. "By 'whale horn' you are referring to the narwhal tusk chalice?"

Kaden offers a minuscule head nod.

"And did you set up the real-life meeting?"

"Yeah, sure." Kaden leans forward and taps his finger on the table for emphasis. "Like, I didn't even go to that meeting, okay? I set it up, whatever. But Klang is the one who met with her. She gave him the horn thing."

"The evidence we have supports that claim. However, I'm far more interested to know how the cup came into the possession of the man you knew as Rory Bombay."

Kaden swallows and leans back. "You mean the guy in the lineup?"

Sheriff Harper nods once.

Kaden crosses his arms tightly and curls his shoulders forward. "Yeah, that guy was weird, man. He offered me a lot of money, and, you know, Klang was already dead. It's not like he needed the cup, right?"

So, that was definitely Rory's partially masked energy I felt in the back room at the antiquities shop. He was holed up there doing research, and I almost caught him.

Erick summarizes the witness's statement, and Kaden confirms that he took the chalice from the top left-hand drawer of Professor Klang's desk—right where Silas left it. Kaden insists he dropped it at the store in Grand Falls and some woman gave him cash. He claims "lineup guy," as he calls him, wasn't at the drop.

Sheriff Harper stands and opens the door. "You're free to go, Mr. Soder. We'll be in touch if we need anything further. Leave your home address with the deputy at the front desk in case we need to contact you over Thanksgiving break."

Kaden unfolds himself from the chair and skulks out without another word.

Standing in the hallway between the observation room and Erick's office, I overhear the sheriff instructing Johnson to prep Frank Freeman for transport to the county jail, where he will undergo a complete battery of medical tests and a psychological evaluation. Sounds like the cursory examination he received from the paramedics last night indicated a type of amnesia, resulting from a severe blow to the head.

Guilty as charged. I whacked him senseless with a ten-pound block of ice, and I'd do it again in a similar situation. He threatened to take two lives; I handled the situation, without taking any.

I step back into the observation room and wait for Erick. I don't want to get caught eavesdropping.

The amnesia diagnosis should assuage the fears of all the laypeople involved in the investigation. Silas Willoughby and I are the only ones who know the truth. Well, and Grams and Pyewacket, of course.

Erick opens the door and steps into the observation room. "I asked Frank every question I could think of and I'd have to say the amnesia is real. There's no trace of Rory Bombay."

Nodding my head, I breathe a sigh of relief. "There's no permanent brain damage, right?"

"Whatever you did was in self-defense. There's been absolutely no mention of any charges. He hasn't even asked for a lawyer."

"Will you be able to get some additional trace evidence from the laundry cart or the freezer doors?"

"We have a team over there checking everything, including the dumpsters. Johnson found the combination lock from my locker in the trunk of Bombay's, or, rather, Freeman's car. That places him in the locker room and explains how he got my jersey."

"You didn't throw a bloody jersey in the cart to get washed?" I raise an eyebrow and scrunch up my face in concern.

He looks at the floor and bites his lip. "It's a weird superstition. As long as we keep winning, I don't wash the jersey."

"Disgusting, but all right." I shiver as I imagine the stench wafting off that thing. "That's further proof that your jersey would never have been conveniently lying on top of the pile of laundry, where Paulsen found it."

He nods. "We're dusting the freezers for prints and we've got Clyde McClintock coming in to see if he can pick Freeman out of a lineup. According to his statement, two different men visited the farm and asked about the artifacts. Professor Klang wanted permission to launch a full-scale archaeological dig, but the other man didn't give a name and was solely interested in the torc."

"That's the one thing I don't understand."

Erick leans against the one-way glass and crosses his arms over his chest in that yummy way that makes his biceps bulge. "There's just *one* thing you don't understand?"

"For now. Why didn't McClintock authorize the dig?"

He nods as though he had been thinking the same thing. "I think Ainsley may have accidentally shed some light on that. She claims that the man who attacked her mother didn't simply move on with the rest of the seasonal workers. Of course, she was a toddler at the time of the actual attack, but it was the arguments she overheard as a young girl that caused her to doubt her parents' story."

"Are you saying there's more than artifacts buried at the Divine Dairy?" I chuckle.

Erick nods and tilts his head. "We'll have to piece together a few more things before we can get a warrant, but I'm certain we'll find that a body was buried somewhere on that property within the last seventeen years."

"Now, that makes sense. Clyde wouldn't want a team of archaeologists scouring the property for artifacts or evidence of a Norse settlement, when he had evidence of something far more incriminating tucked away." I tap my finger to my temple and he grins.

Erick uncrosses his arms and offers me his hand.

I accept, and he pulls me close. "Thanks for never giving up on me, Moon."

Leaning in, I tilt my head up toward his full lips. "I keep my word, Sheriff. When Mitzy Moon takes a case, she doesn't quit until it's solved."

He leans down, brushes the tip of his nose to mine. "You seriously didn't suspect me for one second?"

"Are we being totally honest?"

His breath is warm on my lips. "I think I've mentioned that we're moving into that phase of our relationship."

I struggle to ignore the weakening in my knees. "There was a part of me that wondered, but only for a second, and it was a teensy tine-ty part. Hardly worth mentioning."

His kiss is warm and inviting.

My heart flutters and my tummy flip-flops.

The door blasts open and Deputy Johnson stammers hopelessly.

Erick blushes like a radish and I look everywhere except at people.

I'm the first to recover vocal abilities. "Well, I gotta get busy with storm prep and whatnot." I didn't say it was an amazing segue.

Sheriff Harper nods officially and Johnson steps out of my way.

I pause in the hallway and catch a tidbit about Clyde positively identifying Frank. My work here is done.

Time for me to head over to the Piggly Wiggly and stock up on canned goods, dry goods, toilet paper, bottled water, and, most of all, coffee—exactly like I wrote in that Letter from the Editor.

The storm is scheduled to obliterate the entire Great Lakes area on Thanksgiving day. Weather advisories are encouraging folks to leave a day early, if possible, or cancel their plans entirely. No one should be traveling on Thanksgiving.

I'll believe it when I see it.

CHAPTER 21

As I WATCH Erick carefully guiding his mother over the uneven cobblestone pathway leading to Twiggy's front door, my heart swells with pride and love. How anyone in their right mind could have thought for one second that this man was responsible for murder is beyond even my vast imagination.

The door of the two-story Arts and Crafts, prairie-style home opens and two dogs burst forth.

I tighten my grip on the precious apple and pumpkin pies.

One pup is tan and compact. He sports a holiday sweater, festooned with fall leaves and pumpkins. The other is a massive Husky with piercing blue eyes, thick blue-black fur, and a white belly.

"Bartles and Jaymes, sit." Twiggy's stern command receives an instant response.

Two puppers plant their bottoms on either side of the walkway. The smaller one whimpers and fights the urge to assault the guests with tail wags and tongue licks.

Erick waves. "Twiggy, you know my mom, Gracie, right?"

"Sure do. I hate to admit it, Gracie, but I wasn't sorry when you quit playing bingo. You had an unnatural lucky streak that severely interfered with my winnings."

Gracie laughs warmly and clutches Erick's arm. "Well, you know how Ricky worries about me when I'm out after dark."

Chuckling at my favorite nickname for Sheriff Harper, I stop between the two obedient dogs. "Am I allowed to pet them?"

Twiggy descends the short run of steps from her porch and skirts around the Harpers. She steps up beside the smaller dog and makes an "okay" symbol with her left hand. "Say hello, Jaymes." She swings the symbol toward me. Jaymes instantly rises on his back legs and waves his right paw manically.

"You better take the pies. You know how uncoordinated I can be."

She rescues the pastry perfection, and I immediately reach down and shake his adorable brown paw. "Pleased to meet you, Jaymes."

By this time Bartles is whining, and his little rear end is twitching with anticipation.

Jaymes drops onto all fours and Twiggy gives Bartles the signal. "Say hello to Mitzy."

The black Husky rises on his hind legs, and when he wiggles his right paw, it nearly reaches my shoulder. I shake it hastily. "Pleased to meet you, Bartles."

He drops and the two dogs chase each other around the yard as Twiggy and I head indoors.

"They are really well behaved."

Twiggy tilts her head. "What did you expect, doll?"

"Touché."

The multiple banks of narrow, vertical windows flood the neutral décor with northern light, and the open-plan kitchen/dining area is a bustle of activity. Odell has taken over the cooking, and the much-recovered Amaryllis is pouring wine for everyone. A luscious mélange of roasting turkey and bubbling gravy fills the space, making my mouth water.

Silas appears next to me and whispers, "How is Isadora?"

"Furious. She gave a lengthy speech about never imagining she'd be treated more unfairly in death than in life."

He snickers. "Good thing she can't leave that bookshop, eh?"

My fervent nod agrees. "This sweater is punishment enough."

He inspects my colorful autumnal fashion and struggles to hide his grin. "Very festive."

Rolling my eyes, I reply, "That's one word for it." I grasp his arm as he moves away. "Did you find a proper home for the torc?"

"The artifacts were purchased by an anonymous collector, on behalf of the *Norwegian government*, I believe." He places one hand on his rounded belly and chuckles.

My eyes spark with worry. "Did Frank get his 'Rory' memory back? Is Rory the anonymous collector? That doesn't seem like something to joke about."

Silas smooths his mustache with a thumb and forefinger and his eyes twinkle with the immense power lurking beneath his unassuming exterior. "The torc will remain safe in my vault. Now that we know its true power, we must protect it from those who would twist it toward darkness. The chalice, along with the balance of the items, will form the core of a Norse Expansion in North America exhibit, which will be augmented as additional artifacts are unearthed." He nods toward Erick. "The sheriff has agreed to cooperate with a team of archeologists to conduct a search of the Divine Dairy's acreage for the alleged modern-day corpse."

Gracie Harper releases her hold on her son's arm and accepts a glass of wine.

"Just one, Mom. You know you're not supposed to mix alcohol with your medication." Erick shakes his head.

She shrugs innocently and introduces herself to my father as he nods politely and slips by to greet me.

"This was a great idea, Mitzy. It's nice to spend this holiday of gratitude with all the people we care about." His eyes dart lovingly toward Amaryllis before he pulls me into a warm hug.

"It is, Dad. Glad we found a way to make things work, even if Grams will hold it against us for all eternity!"

Erick pats Jacob on the back, and they exchange a handshake. "Is it just me, Jacob, or does she spend an awful lot of time talking about a woman she supposedly never met?" His blue eyes sparkle with mischief.

My father expertly avoids the loaded question and instead offers his own teasing banter. "Welcome to the Frequent Felons Club, Harper. My daughter and I are founding members."

Erick blushes, shakes his head, and looks down at

his own feet. "I had that coming. After spending a little time on the other side of the bars, I have a new appreciation for my freedom and a new understanding for people who are in the wrong place at the wrong time."

My father claps a hand onto Erick's shoulder and looks him in the eye. "Hey, I deserved what I got—mostly. I made some bad choices and some even worse friends, but you're a decent guy, through and through. Paulsen should've known better."

Erick shrugs. "She was doing her job. I would've made the same choice if our roles had been reversed."

And as though the mere speaking of her name summons her, the front door opens and in waddles Paulsen and—

Leaning toward Erick, I rise onto my tiptoes and whisper, "Who is that with Paulsen?"

He looks down at me as though I've gone insane. "Her husband. Greg Finley."

You could've used a forklift to pick my chin up off the floor. "She has a husband?"

Erick elbows me. "Behave."

Paulsen approaches me with slightly less than her usual disdain. "Greg, this is Mitzy Moon."

Greg sizes me up, looks at Erick, and looks back at me, before extending a hand. "Pauly's told me lots about you."

Oh, the things I wish I could say. Instead, I give his hand a friendly shake. "Nice to meet you, Greg." The conversation opener falls flat, since out of the corner of my eye, my attention is pulled toward a surprising spectacle.

Twiggy steps up onto the piano bench. Yes, she has a piano! She clinks her wineglass with a fork.

Once the room settles down, she proceeds. "Now that everyone's here, I'd like to make a toast. To the friends we make and the family we choose. May we meet for half an hour in heaven before the devil knows we're dead!"

"Hear! Hear!" Odell raises his glass.

Obligatory clinking of glasses passes through the gathering of friends, and Wayne reaches up to support Twiggy as she jumps down from her perch. Jacob smoothly moves in next to her and attempts to whisper, but even I can hear him as he asks, "Can we turn on the game?"

Twiggy throws back the rest of her wine and replies to all. "The game is on in the rec room. And Wayne here will make drinks for anyone needin' somethin' stronger than grape juice. What time are we eatin', Odell?"

He opens the oven, lifts a few lids from the pots on the stove, and glances at the clock. "Dinner in two hours. Don't be late, or Mitzy will eat all the mashed potatoes."

The room erupts in far more laughter than I feel is necessary.

Amaryllis and I help set the table and arrange the trivets on the sideboard, while the rest of the attendees practically sprint to the rec room.

Shouts of "There's beer!" "Look at all these snacks!" and my personal favorite: "A pool table!" can be heard from the dining area.

Amaryllis places the pumpkin pie on a literal pedestal and turns to give me a wink. "That decorative oak leaf and acorn accent in the center reminds me of something." She taps a finger on her lips. "I can't quite—"

I sidle up next to her and hiss, "All right! You found me out. I went to Bless Choux to see if Anne had time to teach me how to make pumpkin pie, but, of course, she's too busy making pumpkin pies for the rest of Pin Cherry to have time to give baking lessons. I thought it would be in everyone's best interest if I simply bought a couple of her delicious pies, rather than potentially expose the group to some type of food poisoning."

Slipping an arm around my shoulders, Amaryllis gives me a squeeze. "Your secret's safe with me. If my options were bake a pie or face the noose, you could say goodbye to this elegant neck." She gestures to her lovely ballerina neck.

We share a laugh, and a little flame flickers in

my heart. I may not be able to spend Thanksgiving with my mother, but I'm definitely warming up to the idea of spending many more with my soon to be step-mom.

Emotions are bubbling, and I need some air. "Can you handle things in here? I'm gonna step out on the porch for a minute."

She smiles and kindly ignores the tears threatening at the corners of my eyes. "Take your time. I've got the trivet situation handled."

The crisp air clears my head, as a deer disappears into the birch and pine forest surrounding Twiggy's property.

Leaning against the porch post, I take a sip of wine and smile. The family of my choosing. That sounds like exactly the kind of family I want. These people, this town, these memories—it's all part of a beautiful new life I'm building.

Touching the dream catcher necklace resting on my lurid Thanksgiving sweater, I whisper a message of gratitude to my dear, departed mother. "Happy Thanksgiving, Cora."

And, as if by magic, the first snowflakes fall.

Stretching out my hand, I catch one in my palm and smile as the one-of-a-kind crystal warms to a drop of liquid.

Erick's arms circle around me from behind and I lean back against his chest. "I'm sorry Coraline isn't here to see what a wonderful human being she made. But I'd like to think she's looking down on you from heaven, and she's even prouder than me."

I set my wineglass on the railing and swirl into Erick's embrace. Happy tears trickle down my cheek and, for the first time in more than a decade, I truly am grateful. "I have a lot to be thankful for this year, Sheriff."

"Me too." He kisses me sweetly and gives me a crooked grin. "If this storm lives up to the hype, we might be at Twiggy's for more than a meal."

"You mean we could be snowed in? Overnight? All of us?"

He nuzzles into my neck. "Mmhmm. It's a house full. We'll have to double up, you know. Do you wanna be my bunkmate?"

Gulp.

This promises to be one heck of a Thanksgiving . . .

Come on, winter, hit me with your best shot!

End of Book 10

But, the mysteries continue...
Curl up with the next book in the Mitzy Moon Mysteries series!

A NOTE FROM TRIXIE

Thank you to each and every one of you! Another case solved! I'll keep writing them if you keep reading . . .

The best part of "living" in Pin Cherry Harbor continues to be feedback from my early readers. Thank you to my alpha readers/cheerleaders, Angel and Michael. HUGE thanks to my fantastic beta readers who continue to give me extremely useful and honest feedback: Veronica McIntyre and Nadine Peterse-Vrijhof. And big "small town" hugs to the world's best ARC Team – Trixie's Mystery ARC Detectives!

Another thing I'm truly grateful for is my editor, Philip Newey. I always look forward to Philip's direct, actionable feedback. I'd also like to give some heartfelt thanks to Brooke for her tireless proofreading! Any errors are my own.

FUN FACT: One of the two concussions I received in my lifetime was during a broomball game!

My favorite quote from this case: "I never behave more poorly than when someone tells me to behave well." ~ Grams

I'm currently writing book twelve in the Mitzy Moon Mysteries series, and I think I may just live in Pin Cherry Harbor forever. Mitzy, Grams, and Pyewacket got into plenty of trouble in book one, *Fries and Alibis*. But I'd have to say that book three, *Wings and Broken Things*, is when most readers say the series becomes unputdownable.

I hope you'll continue to hang out with us.

Trixie Silvertale (November 2020)

HOPES AND SLIPPERY SLOPES

Mitzy Moon Mysteries #11

A dangerous race. The peal of wedding bells. Will this psychic sleuth catch a bouquet or a bullet?

Mitzy Moon finally has a chance to spend a normal, murder-free day with family. And she's super-excited to support her legendary snowmobile racer dad as he's honored for his place in the record books. But instead of a celebration on the podium, she finds a corpse under the snow.

With a holiday wedding at her bookshop looming, it's a terrible time to take on a new case and an orphan. Somehow, Mitzy hopes to juggle the investigation, the nuptials, her meddling Ghost-ma, and an interfering feline. But when her new house guest sees something he shouldn't, her secrets start to unravel . . .

Can Mitzy solve the case before midnight strikes, or will her resolution end in tragedy?

Hopes and Slippery Slopes is the eleventh book in the hilarious paranormal cozy mystery series, Mitzy Moon Mysteries. If you like snarky heroines, supernatural misfits, and a dash of romance, then you'll love Trixie Silvertale's twisty whodunit.

Buy *Hopes and Slippery Slopes* to solve a New Year's Eve mystery today!

Grab yours here!
readerlinks.com/l/5212005

Scan this QR Code with the camera on your phone. You'll be taken right to the next case!

Once you're in the Club, you'll also be the first to receive updates from Pin Cherry Harbor and access to giveaways, new release announcements, behind-the-scenes secrets, and much more!

Scan this QR Code with the camera on your phone. You'll be taken right to the page to join the Club!

THANK YOU!

Trying out a new book is always a risk and I'm thankful that you rolled the dice with Mitzy Moon. If you loved the book, the sweetest thing you can do (*even sweeter than pin cherry pie à la mode*) is to leave a review so that other readers will take a chance on Mitzy and the gang.

Don't feel you have to write a book report. A brief comment like, "Can't wait to read the next book in this series!" will help potential readers make their choice.

★★★★★
Leave a quick review HERE
https://readerlinks.com/l/1313027
★★★★★

Thank you kindly, and I'll see you in Pin Cherry Harbor!

Dangers and Empty Mangers

Heists and Poltergeists

Blades and Bridesmaids

Scones and Tombstones

Vandals and Yule Scandals

Harper and Moon Investigations
Paranormal Cozy Mysteries

Ropes and Last Hopes

Bells and Bombshells

Rodeo Clowns and Shakedowns

Stiffs and Petroglyphs

Fatal Wines and Valentines

April Curses and May Hearses

Wheels and Dirty Deals

Scripts and Empty Crypts

Christmas Catastrophe Mysteries
Culinary Cozy Mysteries

Peppermint Cookie Murder

Apple Dumpling Murder

Linzer Cookie Murder

Chocolate Crinkle Cookie Murder

...more to come!

MAGICAL RENAISSANCE FAIRE MYSTERIES

Explore the world of Coriander the Conjurer. A fortune-telling fairy with a heart of gold!

Book 1:

All Swell That Ends Spell – A dubious festival. A fatal swim. Can this fortune-telling fairy herald the true killer?

Book 2:

Fairy Wives of Windsor – A jolly Faire. A shocking murder. Can this furtive fairy outsmart the killer?

Book 3:

Double Double Royal Trouble – When a treat-peddling witch is found dead, will this cursed faire crumble?

Join Sydney Coleman and her unruly ghosts, as they solve mysteries in a truly haunted mansion!

Book 1: ***Moonlight and Mischief*** – She's desperate for a fresh start, but is a mansion on sale too good to be true?

Book 2: ***Moonlight and Magic*** – A haunted Halloween tour seem like the perfect plan, until there's murder...

Book 3: ***Moonlight and Mayhem*** – An unwelcome visitor. A surprising past. Will her fire sale end in smoke?

USA TODAY Bestselling author Trixie Silvertale grew up reading an endless supply of Lilian Jackson Braun, Hardy Boys, and Nancy Drew novels. She loves the amateur sleuths in cozy mysteries and obsesses about all things paranormal. Those two passions unite in all her cozy mysteries, and she's thrilled to write them and share them with you.

When she's not consumed by writing, she bakes to fuel her creative engine and pulls weeds in her herb garden to clear her head (*and sometimes she pulls out her hair, but mostly weeds*).

Greetings are welcome:
trixie@trixiesilvertale.com

facebook.com/TrixieSilvertale

instagram.com/trixiesilvertale

bookbub.com/authors/trixie-silvertale